CLAIRE

BOOK THREE - THE SABELA SERIES

TINA HOGAN GRANT

Copyright © 2020 by Tina Hogan Grant

All rights reserved.

No part of this book may be reproduced in any form or by any electronic or mechanical means, including information storage and retrieval systems, without written permission from the author, except for brief quotation for the use in a book review.

This is a work of fiction. Any names, characters, places, or incidents are products of the author's imagination and used in a fictitious manner. Any resemblance to actual people, places, or events is purely coincidental or fictionalized.

Edited by Crystal Santoro Editorial Services: https://chrissyseditorialservices.org/

Cover Design by T.E.Black Designs – http://www.teblackdesigns.com

Visit The Author's Website

www.tinahogangrant.com

❦ Created with Vellum

CHAPTER 1

Claire

I'm not ashamed to admit that I disowned my family since my brother, Davin, had been arrested and convicted of rape almost two years ago. Sabela had been a victim (yes, there were quite a few—three, in fact.) She was my co-worker, but they fired her because of Davin's doings. My parents continued to be in denial and believed in his innocence. They had enough substantial evidence to convict him. But in my parent's eyes, their first-born and only son, Davin was not capable of committing such crimes—I beg to differ.

I was in the courtroom that day when they sentenced him to fifteen years in jail. I watched, frozen to my seat, as the officers of the court escorted Davin out in handcuffs. I felt no pity, the only embarrassment; he was my brother. My mom sobbed beside me, and I wanted to barf. My dad was no better. He wrapped his arm around my mom and acted like a man, but held back his tears. But he failed when they read the sentence and collapsed against her and buried his head on her shoulder. My parent's acts of weakness embarrassed me; I shook my head in disgust. I had no words for them and left the courtroom abruptly.

I never visited Davin in prison, and I had no intentions, either. In my mind, he doesn't exist. Neither did my parents. I haven't seen them since that day in court. I know that my parents have seen him often, because of the letters I've received from Davin. He told me they visit him once a month on the weekend. It's the reason I refuse to be a part of my parents' lives.

I haven't responded to any of the letters my parents and Davin sent me. My parents tried to contact me through the US Mail since I changed my phone number shortly after I saw them last. To be blatantly honest, I hope my parents gave up. It's been two months since I received a letter. They used to write to me every month.

Davin still writes, though. I get a letter from him almost every other week—well, what else is there to do in jail other than harass your little sister. I read them once and then throw them away—but I may stop reading them soon. They're not pleasant, and each one gets nastier, and dare I say threatening. I think he's called me every name under the sun and has the nerve to ask how Sabela is—is he for real? Why would he ask me about her? Sabela and I were never close friends, and even if we were, I'd never give him any information. It sounds like he's just fishing. But now his letters hold an unfamiliar tone, a threatening one. In the last one, he wrote—*You are my sister Claire, and you can't change it. I won't disappear so easily. Once I'm out, you will see me again. You can count on it.* Like all the others, I tossed it in the trash, but this one left a mark. Should I worry? I received that letter almost two weeks ago—if he keeps to his schedule, another should arrive any day now.

I'm sure by the time he gets out—which shouldn't be for at least another five to seven years with time served; I will have moved on to somewhere else. Hopefully, somewhere far away. I don't plan on living in this apartment for the rest of my life.

Even behind bars, Davin can do no wrong. Apparently, I am the jerk, according to the many letters I have received not only from Davin—who tells me and I quote; *I shouldn't be acting this way because I am his sister and that no matter what he did, I should be on his side. We are family, and you can't change that!* Excuse me! Be on his side?

My parents have written only to tell me what an embarrassment I am. They have this crazy idea that we should all stick together and show Davin some support. They can all go to hell.

When I was growing up, my parents favored Davin. He was their dream boy, and what Davin wanted, Davin got. No one ever told him no. I think Sabela might have been the first when she said she wouldn't go to Texas with him. His reaction was to go to California, stalk her, and try to rape her.

I must admit, When Sabela started dating Davin, I wasn't happy. She used to work at the dental office. She's drop-dead gorgeous and seemed way out of Davin's league. Everything about her is perfect, from her luscious long brown hair, her seductive dark brown eyes, and her perfectly toned body. I was certain Davin would end up getting hurt big time. Having been under the protective wing of our parents, they didn't allow him to grow up. I never understood what Sabela saw in him—maybe it was his wacky sense of humor. I know how much he made her laugh.

It shocked me when they moved in together and quickly too. But I'm sure Davin wouldn't take no for an answer. I questioned myself. Davin was leaving for the university in Texas. It's obvious now that he had no intention of giving up Sabela. Boy, was I wrong to think he'd be the one to get hurt?

By the time he was a teenager, and before he entered high school, Davin's future had been laid out. He studied at Rice University and would someday become a successful doctor or surgeon.

So when I told my parents my plans, it horrified them. I wanted to go to community college to study to be a dental x-ray technician. I saw the pedestal they put Davin on and their high expectations of him. I wanted no part of that. I didn't want the constant pressures from them in my life. For me, community college was the perfect solution.

When college began, and I needed to live closer, my parents still did what most parents do. When I found a studio apartment, they paid my way until I found a part-time job at a nearby restaurant. I'm twenty-four now and have my degree in college. I recently upgraded to a two-bedroom apartment in the same building, and it's just me and my two-year-old Yorkshire Terrier, Tilly.

I enjoy my job as an x-ray technician. Being in the public eye wasn't for me. At work, I have my little room with my x-ray machine, and it's perfect. The only words spoken between the patient and me are *open wide, bite down,* or *hold your breath*. I don't dress up or wear a lot of make-up. Smock and pants suit me just fine.

When I'm at home, I wear my comfortable baggy sweats. I was never the girlie girl type, and I don't feel attractive. It's another reason I disappointed mom and dad. I rarely wear make-up, except maybe some lip gloss on some rare occasions. I found the easiest way to deal with my hair is to keep it short, so I don't style it every day.

Part of the reason why I've never felt pretty is that since the age of seven, I've had to wear glasses. The name-calling at school—four eyes and many more that I'd rather not repeat have done little for my self-esteem. My mom tried to get me to wear contacts when I turned sixteen, but shit, they hurt like hell, and I flat out refused.

I avoided boys like the plaque to the point they accused me of being gay. In high school, I dated a few guys and lost my virginity to one. And as I expected, I never saw him again. So until recently, I was content with just me and Tilly. That is until Travis entered my life a few months ago, and things have never been the same since.

CHAPTER 2

CLAIRE

Travis found me sobbing in my car one day when I left for my lunch. It embarrassed me. I hadn't seen him approach my vehicle and didn't realize how loud I cried. He checked on me. My beat-up car had broken down yet again, and I had just about had enough. I'd used up all my triple-A tow points. There was no way I could afford to get it fixed. I didn't know what to do.

I'd seen Travis on occasions when he came into work to pick up his girlfriend, Jill. She worked at the front desk. He seemed like a pleasant guy. If I was in the lobby, he nodded and smiled, followed by a hi. He would ask how my day went. My answer was a simple "fine" before I scurried off to return to the safety of my room.

Jill was a different story. Let's just say I tolerated her because we worked in the same office. We didn't have much in common. Her obsession with pink drove me crazy. I hated that color. She wore more bling-bling than a goddamn Christmas tree. I owned three pieces of jewelry. And then there was her need to check herself in a mirror every ten minutes, which I found annoying. I knew she was high maintenance, and I imagined she would be a lot of work for any guy to take on. I often wondered what she and Travis had in common. What did they do together? Did Travis ever ride in her hot pink Mustang?

Travis was my knight in shining armor that day in the parking lot. Not only did he pay to have my car fixed, but he took me out for lunch. I never paid much attention to him before since he was Jill's boyfriend. But man, something happened between us that day. There was a connection like I'd never felt before. It was weird in a way because it didn't matter to me that he had a girlfriend. What ignited between the two of us strengthened my consciousness. In the beginning, it had nothing to do with sex; it was sharing our feelings, emotions, and whatever else we found to talk about at that time. To my surprise, it was a lot. I discovered I could open up to Travis about anything. He also taught me to listen to my heart again, which I had done every time our eyes had met. The elevated heartbeat that occurred repeatedly was an unfamiliar sensation that I didn't want to forget.

That afternoon, I had poured my heart out to him over dinner while we waited for my car. I told him about my financial situation, which turned into bringing up my family troubles. I shared my concerns about work and how I thought no one liked me. Looking back, I'm surprised Travis didn't run. I was a messed up chick that day. But instead of running, he calmed me down. The gentle touch of his masculine hand rested on mine soothed me every time I got upset.

I don't know how many times I apologized for my warped behavior, but he didn't shift or criticize me. He listened and comforted me through his words. I had not experienced something like this before, not even from my parents growing up. They never gave me words of encouragement or told me I'm beautiful. Travis couldn't tell me enough.

I sensed Travis was at ease talking to me about his troubles too. He seemed relaxed when he spoke, and his tone was mellow. He didn't hesitate as the words flowed freely, and I listened, giving him an occasional smile. He opened up about him and Jill—in all honesty, I hadn't thought about her since we had sat down. It wasn't until he told me they had become estranged. He said to me he hadn't been happy in a long time, and I remember feeling a twinge of jealousy and disappointment. *"Oh, I almost forgot you are Jill's boyfriend."* I had said.

"I'm not sure if I can call myself that anymore. We've been leading separate lives for a while now." His confession immediately erased all the insecurities I had. I had no reason to feel jealous. My spirits lifted with the thought that maybe we could see each other again after that night.

When his friend called a few hours later to let us know my car was ready, I wasn't excited as I should have been. I didn't want to leave. I had been drawn to Travis like a magnet and had no desire to go home and return to my lonely world. I saw the disappointment on Travis's face after he hung up his phone. I mirrored his sadness.

We took our time walking back to my car. It took forty-five minutes. Unaware that my car was in their parking lot, I called my work to let them know the repairs were taking longer than expected, and I would be there shortly.

A few minutes from work, we stopped again because Travis wanted to exchange numbers. I reveled at the idea and gave him a warm smile as we stood close and touched elbows to punch in the numbers on our phones.

When we reached my car, I stalled and dangled my keys. For the first time, we found ourselves lost for words.

It wasn't until Jill came out of the office and approached us did I feel uncomfortable. I stood a little too close to Travis but stepped away to give them their space. It was obvious they didn't need it. Neither one smiled at each other or showed any kind of affection towards one another. Their stares were frigid, and their lips were tight.

Jill extended her arm, "here are the keys." Jill snarled at Travis. She placed her hands on her hips and gave him a hard stare. "I'd appreciate it if you'd try to remember to take your house keys in the morning and not bug me at work." She snapped.

Travis rolled his eyes and shook his head. He yanked the keys from her hand and matched her tone when he spoke. "I couldn't find them because you took them off my truck key chain when you couldn't find yours. So don't blame me."

"I don't have time for this." Jill snapped again and had abruptly turned around and marched off.

"See what I mean," Travis said as Jill disappeared into the building. "There's no love lost there."

After I had thanked Travis for his help and shared an awkward goodbye, I reluctantly pulled myself away from his company and returned to work. I avoided Jill at all costs. But Travis had left his mark. Over the next few weeks, he was a permanent fixture in my brain. I couldn't shake him. I saw him in my dreams. I sang songs to him in my car on the way to work. Often I would catch myself daydreaming about him at work. He had become my new distraction in my everyday life, and for the first time, I brought myself to orgasm while thinking about him alone in my bed.

I became even more distant from Jill. Many mornings she'd walk into work, slam down her purse and complain about Travis. But her complaints revolved around her and what he wasn't doing for her. He never took her out; he never bought her flowers. He refused to buy the dress she wanted because it was too expensive. I couldn't stand to listen to her harsh bashings of Travis and soon left whenever they began. It was clear she didn't know Travis at all. How could you live with someone you don't know? I didn't understand it.

There were so many times I wanted to call him and let him know I couldn't stop thinking about him. Hours went by, where I sat on my couch alone. I hugged my dog Tilly while I stared at my phone. But I couldn't bring myself to do it. No matter how much I wanted to be with him, he was involved with Jill. My other fear was rejection. I don't know if I could have handled that. For now, I could keep him in my life through my dreams, my songs, and whatever else I could conjure up.

But it seemed I had been on Travis's mind, too. One night while I was fixing my usual dinner for one in my apartment, he surprised me with a phone call. I froze when I saw his name flashing on the screen, and my heart skipped a beat. Jill popped into my head, and I questioned whether to answer the call. But my desires to hear his husky voice were stronger than my resistance, and I inhaled deeply before picking up the phone.

"Hello," I whispered as I picked up Tilly, who was sitting at my feet, waiting for handouts. I held her under my arms and headed over to the couch.

"Hi, Claire. It's Travis."

I closed my eyes briefly. I felt my heart flutter from the sound of his masculine voice.

"Hi, Travis." I didn't know what else to say. I waited for him to break the uncomfortable silence that followed.

After a few seconds, he opened the conversation. "I hope I'm not calling too late. I can't stop thinking about you."

I stroked Tilly as I spoke. "I'm having the same problem. I can't stop thinking about you either." I confessed.

"Can I see you?" Travis asked in a serious tone.

I glanced around my apartment. It was a mess, but I could make it look decent in about fifteen minutes.

"Now?" I asked.

"If that's okay," he hesitated. "Maybe we could meet for a drink. I'm sitting in my truck and don't want to go home."

I scanned my apartment again and released a sigh of relief, knowing I wouldn't have to do a flash cleaning. "Sure, that would be great. I've not eaten dinner yet. How about somewhere that serves food too?" I laughed.

But the call didn't end there. We stayed on the phone for

another hour, catching up on the last two weeks. Conversation with Travis came naturally. "Listen, as much as I love talking to you; I could have eaten dinner by now. Let me get changed, and we can pick up where we left off when I meet you."

Travis laughed down at the phone. "You're right. I can't wait to see you." I sensed the smile in his voice and broke out in a smile of my own. "See you soon." He said before hanging up.

After ending the call, I blushed and giggled like a high school student. No one had ever asked me out on a prom date, but I'm sure this is how it would have felt. I let out a scream and jumped up off the couch. I danced around the apartment, kicking my bare heels high in the air. With a dying urge to break out into a song, I grabbed my phone and synced it to my speakers and told Siri to play "Feel Like Making Love" by Bad Company.

With the music blasting, I roared out the lyrics and danced around my bedroom while scrambling for something to wear. I grabbed a pair of jeans, trainers, and a white sweatshirt. After glancing at myself in the bathroom mirror and applying some lip gloss, I gave my short hair a vigorous shake. Satisfied with my casual attire, I left some lights on and said goodbye to Tilly, who was curled up on the couch. Sitting next to her was my backpack and phone, which I grabbed before heading out the door.

CHAPTER 3

TRAVIS

I might have been in the wrong when I called Claire. I hadn't broken up with Jill yet, but jeez, I wanted to hear kind words for a change. I needed to be in the company of someone who appreciated me. Jill's words were harsh and full of hatred. Claire showed only compassion and kindness when I had been with her.

I didn't have to think about it before I called her. It seemed like it was the right thing to do. I'd just gotten off the phone with Jill—well, actually, I hung up on her. I couldn't take much more of her insults and the demeaning way she spoke to me. People have talked to their dogs better than she has spoken to me. I held my tongue as I listened to her tell me how boring I was. She complained that I never took her anywhere. And when she snarled that she would go out with her girlfriends, I felt relieved. Sorry, Jill, but the last few times we had gone out had not been fun. Each time you stormed off and took a cab home. If I remember correctly, one time, you left abruptly when I ordered red wine instead of white, and you thought the world had ended.

As soon as I heard Claire's voice over the phone, I broke into a smile. Jill had quickly become a distant memory. My world was a happier place when Claire was in it. I hadn't smiled since the last time I saw her. Before I started the truck, I glanced in the rearview mirror and raked my fingers through my hair.

I arrived first and happy to see there wouldn't be a wait. The host grabbed a few menus and showed me to a quiet booth. He asked if I would like a drink while I waited.

"Sure. A Coors Light." I replied.

Within a few minutes, he returned with my drink. Claire soon followed to join me. I beamed her a magnificent smile. She returned one and quickened her pace.

She slid into the booth across from me. Her eyes were bright and matched her smile. "Hi," She said in a pleasant tone that I had yearned to hear.

I smiled back, admiring every inch of her. God, it felt good to see her. "Hi," I said. "You look great."

Claire glanced down at her wardrobe and laughed while adjusting her black-framed eyeglasses. "You're kidding, right?"

"No, I mean it. You look beautiful."

Claire laughed again. "Okay, I think you're the one that needs glasses."

The waiter interrupted us. "Can I get you something to drink?" He asked Claire.

"Yes, please. I'll take a bud light."

"So, how have you been?" I asked as the waiter walked away. "And how is your car holding up?"

"I've been good, and the car is plodding along," she said as she tapped her knuckles on the surface of the table.

I grabbed her hand before she could pull it back. "I've missed you."

Claire looked down at our hands that were entwined together. She raised her head and looked my way, "I've missed you too." She released a nervous laugh. "This is weird, Travis. You're with Jill, and yet here we are meeting for dinner." She let go of my hand and leaned back against the booth and giggled. "You should have seen me after I hung up the phone. I danced around my apartment as if I were a high school kid. Even my dog Tilly looked at me with confused eyes."

I watched as she lightly moistened her lips with her tongue and continued to speak. "Funny thing is, Jill never entered my mind. The only thing I cared about was you called. I couldn't wait to see you, Travis. But now that I'm here, Jill is the first thing that's popping into my head."

I understood her concern. It felt weird for me too, but when I saw Claire again, I realized I had no future with Jill. "I told you, Jill and I don't get along. We hardly speak to each other anymore," I said with a slight kick to my tone.

Claire rested her forearms on the table and clasped her hands together. "I know. But you're still with her, and I don't want to be the person who comes between you. What if there's a chance you guys can fix whatever is wrong in your relationship?"

Claire's honesty made her attractive. She was raw and told you how it was, even if it risks her getting hurt. I shook my head and cradled my hands over hers. "Oh, Claire, trust me. It won't happen. It's over. I needed to find the courage to tell her. I don't want a scene. I need to find the right time where we can talk like two adults." I raised my hands and tilted my head hastily. "Or maybe she will end it first?" I squeezed her hands and reached for the menu. "Now come on—enough of Jill. I'm sure you're starving. Let's order some food and enjoy each other's company."

Claire gave me a smile that warmed my heart and took a large sip of her beer that the waiter had dropped off, "Okay."

While we sat in silence and read the menus, I found myself distracted by Claire's presence. It was hard to focus on the task at hand and decide on what to eat. Periodically, my eyes would wander and sneak a peek at Claire. I knew she didn't see it, but her beauty mesmerized me. She wore no makeup, but she didn't need to. Her eyelashes were naturally thick, and it brought out the sharp navy color of her eyes. That's how perfect she is. The skin on her face doesn't have a single blemish. It's flawless and a perfect light honey shade.

I tried to hide my elevated quick breaths caused by the admiration I had for her. Her short brown hair glistened beneath the lights which hung over the table. I laughed when she confessed she didn't know what to do with it. A good shake and natural air-dry works fine, she said. I could never imagine Claire with a top-notch hairstyle or lengthy hair that would hide her beautiful face. Her hairstyle might be simple, but it suited her face perfectly. I especially liked how the ends curled up slightly just below her jawline.

Her thin black-framed glasses added to her sexiness and magnified her brilliant navy eyes. I could stare at her all day. She mesmerized me.

When we first met, I knew straight away she had low self-esteem. I planned on changing that if she continued to see me. When she looks in the mirror, I want her to see what I see. It crushed me when I had to sit in silence and listen to her complain about her imperfections. Her biggest problem was her body and how it wasn't perfect or had the curves like Sabela and Jill's. No matter what I said, she shook her head in disagreement and insisted I was complimenting her to make her feel better. It wasn't the case.

I couldn't speak for Sabela, but Jill spent more time in front of the goddamn mirror and watched her calories more than she talked to me. And then there's our bathroom, which has double sinks, but two-thirds of the counter is full of her crap. She has tubes of creams for her face, legs, and aging. There are other miscellaneous items. Why would a woman need so many? It's crazy. She has hair, dryers, combs, brushes, and hair clips spread out everywhere. And let's not forget the nail polish, jewelry, and perfume bottles. Every day she spends hours sitting in front of the mirror and then more time in front of another mirror that makes her face look huge! She wasted so much time in front of a goddamn mirror instead of doing something productive or something meaningful.

Jill spent an hour a night at the gym, four nights a week after work. Yeah, her body is toned in all the right places, I won't deny it, but my god the hours she spends to keep in shape makes me wonder if it's worth all the effort. She could do so much more in life that would be much more enjoyable. I swear she takes vain to a whole different level.

Claire may not have the curves or tight body that Jill has, but to me, she is far sexier. She's not tall. Her 5'6" frame had little meat on it, but she looked healthier than the tall, skinny, malnourished models splashed across the covers of magazines. I love her broad shoulders and how she holds her back straight when she walks. It represented the vibrant woman that she is, and I must admit I love how her confident strides highlight her small perky breasts.

I soon realized after I had met Claire, who is genuine and refreshing, how too much vanity can make a person ugly. Looks didn't run Claire's life, but she compared herself to others. She wasn't going to let it drive her, though. Unlike Jill, whose only hobby is herself, Claire had interests that I would love to share with her someday. I've never had a girl that hiked, camped, kayaked, and even fished. Sadly, she's done them all alone, but that tells me she is not afraid of her own company. What a gift that is. I only wish Claire would realize it too. Maybe one day I'll be able to convince her.

After spending a few minutes going over the menu, the waiter returned, and we placed our orders. Claire decided on fish and chips, and I went with a cheeseburger. As soon as he left, Claire talked about her brother Davin. "I got another letter from Davin the other day," she said in a somber tone.

I knew Davin when he dated Sabela. In fact, Jill and I had hung out with them a few times before he snapped. I thought I knew the guy. He seemed okay, but it turned out I didn't. I can't blame Claire for cutting all ties with him, but I have mixed feelings for her parents. I've stepped lightly when the topic has come up, leaving subtle hints that maybe she should try to make amends with her mom and dad because she may regret it later in life, but she quickly shrugged it off by telling me I didn't understand.

I know it left her scarred, and I worry she is fearful of Davin. I see it in her eyes when she's talked about him. Maybe she's not ready to discuss it, and that's okay, I'm not going anywhere, and I will be here when she is. She can't avoid her parents forever. One day she's going to have to talk to them, and I will support her in every way I can.

My lips narrowed, and I clenched my jaw at the mention of Davin's name. "What did he say?" I asked.

Claire folded her arms across her chest. "Oh, the same stuff as always. That I should show him support like mom and dad are doing." Her eyes darkened, and she looked worried as she spoke.

I tried to comfort her with my words. "Claire, he can't do anything to you while he is in jail. He will be there for at least another five years, if not longer. Who knows where you will be by then." I leaned forward and reached for her hand that she cradled across her chest and held it tight. "Don't worry, okay."

She looked my way and nodded. Claire returned the squeeze to my hand, but I had a gut feeling I hadn't convinced her.

"I know. His letters just hurt. That's all." She leaned back, tossing her head back across the booth. "This is so twisted that even my parents have turned against me." She raised her voice a notch. "He's the bad guy, not me. I can't fucking believe it. I can't believe they are taking his side over mine after what he did." She gave me a hard stare and took my hand again. "I can't be their daughter if they continue to support him." She shook her head in disgust. "I just won't," she said with force.

"I understand where you're coming from, but maybe your parents are hurting too. I'm not sticking up for them, just stating a fact as far as the letters from Davin go. Don't read them. Just throw them away." I paused and shifted in my seat. She had confided in me that she missed her parents. They let her down, and she believed she could never forgive them. "Have your parents written?" I asked.

"No, not for a while. Maybe they gave up. I know I moved, but I'm in the same complex. The mailman has been putting all my mail in my new box. If they had written me letters, I would have gotten it." She looked over at me with sad eyes and sounded sincere when she spoke. "If I could fix the relationship with my parents, believe me, I would, but because they continue to visit and keep Davin in their lives, there's no way it can happen."

I nodded and then leaned back when the waiter approached the table with our food. The scent of the cooked burger invaded my nose, and I inhaled deeply. "Damn, I'm starving. Thanks for suggesting a place that serves food. I didn't realize I was so hungry." I laughed.

The delicious-looking food in front of us was reason enough to drop the subject of Davin. We talked about more pleasant things, and the mood lightened. Claire's smile soon returned when I confessed to her how much I enjoyed her company. Together we raised our glasses to our newfound friendship.

With our bellies full and three beers later, we leaned back in our seats, feeling content while the waiter removed our plates.

"Can I get you any desserts?" The waiter asked.

Claire and I shook our heads while holding our stomachs. "Oh god, no, we're too full," I replied.

I took the last swig of my beer and gave Claire a smug smile. "You know I'm not ready to say good night to you yet. What do you want to do now?" I asked, hoping she didn't want to say goodnight either.

She didn't answer me right away, which had me worried. Instead, she took the last sip of her drink and gave me a stare. I waited patiently for her reply, not taking my eyes off her as she set her glass down and gave me a subtle smile with her eyes narrowed. "We could go back to my place and watch a movie," she said with a hint of nervousness. "Tilly's probably wondering where I am. I'm usually always home in the evenings."

I creased my brow, "Tilly?"

Claire let out a cute laugh. "My dog."

"Oh yeah. I forgot you had a dog." The fact she had invited me back to her place got me excited. Yes, I wanted to feel the warmth of her lips against mine and inhale her scent. The thought of peeling off her clothes and seeing her naked for the first time had me aroused. I was ready to take her, but I'm going to let Claire hold the cards on that one. I will wait. The last thing I want to do is scare her away before we've even established a relationship. Which is what I honestly want? I'm just not sure if she does or will with Jill still in the picture. I know I need to end it with Jill. She must know our relationship has run its course, just like I do. I suddenly realized I got sidetracked, and it had ruined my mood. I shook my head to snap myself out of my negative thoughts and noticed Claire waited for my answer.

I reassured her with a smile. "I would love to go to your place."

Claire cocked her head to one side and beamed me her pearly white perfect teeth. "Great! You can follow me in your truck, and I'll show you where to park."

CHAPTER 4

CLAIRE

I'm not sure if asking Travis back to my place was the best idea, but I couldn't ignore the chemistry I felt between us. Just being in his presence sent my heart racing, and I wasn't ready to say goodnight. Tonight something happened between us, and I wanted to stay with it and see where it led.

The drive back to my place was only about fifteen minutes. I pointed from my car where Travis could park and then parked my car in the underground parking lot. I told Travis I'd meet him in front of the main gate. I pulled up to the dark, isolated parking structure and turned off the motor. Silence surrounded my mind, and I rubbed my sweaty palms. I was nervous and excited all at the same time. Everything moved so fast. I checked myself in the rearview mirror and spoke to the reflection of my eyes in the mirror. "What are you doing, Claire?" I said with a hard stare. "He's still with Jill." I tilted my head and continued to look at myself in the mirror. "But not for long," I said, followed by a wink at myself.

After I had ended my one-sided conversation, I locked my car and went to meet Travis. Once I turned the corner, I spotted him at the bottom of the steps illuminated by the street lamp. The sight took my breath away, and I paused for a moment to enjoy the view. I couldn't believe that such a handsome man was interested in little old me, especially when he had been dating someone as beautiful as Jill. He stood with his hands in the front pockets of his jeans while looking up at the full moon, beaming in the sky.

He must have heard my footsteps because he turned and looked in my direction, smiled, and pulled out one of his hands to wave. I smiled back at him. The night's chill wrapped its way around my body.

"The temperature dropped quickly, didn't it?" He said as I approached him.

"It did," I replied as I blew into my hands. "Come on, let's go inside."

Travis followed me up the steps and waited while I punched in the code. The door buzzed, and Travis reached around me and pulled it open.

"Thanks," I said, surprised by his gesture.

My condo was at the end of the hallway, and Travis waited as I fumbled with my keys. I heard Tilly barking on the other side. "It's okay, Tilly. It's just mommy." I turned to Travis and shrugged my shoulders. "Surely I'm not the only one that talks to their dogs."

Travis raised his hands. "No comment," he joked.

I opened the door, and Tilly greeted us excitedly. "Hey, girl! I missed you," I said as she ran out into the hallway, shaking her entire body with excitement.

Travis laughed and bent his knees as he held out his hand for Tilly to sniff. We waited for Tilly to accept him before we entered the condo. Tilly continued with her abundance of enthusiasm over an unexpected house guest—which I rarely had and did repetitive jumps on her hind legs while pawing at Travis's jeans as he walked.

"Tilly! Down!" I yelled several times, but she didn't listen.

"It's okay," Travis said with a laugh.

I led him into the living room where the TV was playing

Friends. "Here, have a seat." I turned to face him. "Would you like some coffee? I've had enough beer. I have to work in the morning."

Travis made himself comfortable on the couch, and within minutes, Tilly jumped on his lap and finally relaxed. "Sure, that would be great. Thanks." He scanned the cozy room and smiled at the picture of Tilly above the TV. It was the only photo in the room. The other images were mountain landscapes and a lighthouse. The walls were painted a light beige, and the door trims were painted white. It wasn't a large room, but it didn't seem cramped with the brown leather couch, the coffee table, and the two matching ottomans. To his left was a bookshelf where Travis read a few titles. She had a vast selection of camping and hiking books and a collection of thrillers. Behind the couch were a dining room table and four chairs. "I love your place," he said as he petted Tilly, who was already sound asleep.

I spoke to him from the kitchen as I filled up the coffee machine with water. "Thanks. It's small. But it's just Tilly and me. I recently upgraded to a two-bedroom. Now I have room to store all my hiking and camping gear." I popped my head through the doorway. "You like to camp? Right?"

Travis stretched his arms out across the back of the couch. His beefy biceps that peeked through the sleeves of his grey t-shirt caught my attention, "I used to love it. I've not been in a few years. According to a certain person and we both know who that is, camping is too dirty."

I nodded. "Ahh, gotcha. I went for a weekend to Big Bear before my car broke down. I'm ready for another trip soon."

"You went by yourself?" Travis asked.

After adding the coffee grinds, I turned on the machine and joined him. "Yep. I always go by myself. I'm fine with it." I took a seat next to him, and Tilly jumped in my lap. "It's good for the soul, you know," I said while petting Tilly, who had curled up in a ball."

The coffee machine gurgled, and the pleasant aroma of coffee invaded the room.

"Ah, that coffee smells good," Travis said as he removed his arms from the back of the couch. While he tried not to disturb Tilly, I leaned over and reached for the remote control that sat on the coffee table. "Do you want to watch a movie?" I asked.

"Sure."

I turned to face him and smiled before handing him the control. "Okay, you pick while I get the coffee."

Travis took the remote control. "Okay." He surfed the channels.

Before I left the room, I knelt in front of Travis's and gently picked up Tilly and placed her in her bed on the floor next to the couch. "How do you like your coffee?" I hollered from the kitchen a few minutes later.

"Black. One sugar."

I returned with two mugs of steaming brewed coffee and precariously sat them on the coffee table. Travis leaned forward and held my hand to steady it. His hand was warm as it cradled mine. I raised my eyes and looked into his eyes. "Thank you," I said, followed by a subtle smile while our hands still touched.

He smiled back. "Your welcome."

When the mugs were safely on the table, Travis pulled his hand back. I rubbed my skin, where his hand had touched mine, and took a seat next to him.

"What did you decide on?" I asked while taking a sip from the mug.

"Do you like old movies?" he asked.

I smiled. "I love them."

"How about the Duke?"

"John Wayne?" I shifted in my seat, settling my body into the cushions while trying not to spill my coffee. "Sounds good. The Duke never disappoints me." I laughed.

"Which one is on?"

"The Sons of Katie Elder."

Travis leaned back against the couch and stretched his legs out to the side of the coffee table, revealing his well-defined muscles of his hefty thighs beneath his jeans. I breathed in deeply through my nose to captivate his masculine scent. He lured me in, and I loved everything about him. He was a real man, rugged and strong. His body was lean and hard. It took all my strength not to reach out and touch it. But what I also liked was that he had a compassionate side too. I'd seen it when I had poured my heart out to him, and he listened to me attentively. He was perfect in every way. I can't remember the last time I had felt this attracted to someone.

I wanted to get comfortable and kicked off my tennis shoes. I wedged my body in the corner of the two-seater couch and bent my knees up to my chest.

Travis patted his knee. "You can rest your legs on mine if you'd like. I won't bite." He chuckled. "I don't want you crammed in the corner."

I hesitated for a moment and gave him a subtle smile as I stretched out my legs and laid them across his thick thighs. "Thanks."

A few minutes into the movie, Travis took me by surprise when he squeezed my toes playfully. "You have tiny feet." He wriggled my toes more. "They are so cute."

I laughed and tried to pull away, but he had a firm grip. "Stop. I'm ticklish, you know."

"Really," he said with a mischievous grin before he tickled me again.

I squealed from his touch and released myself out of his hold. "If you keep tickling me, I'll move," I said while trying not to laugh.

Travis grabbed my ankle and pulled my leg onto his lap and patted my shin. "Okay. Okay. I'll stop, I promise."

I tried to focus on the movie but failed miserably. For the next ten minutes, we sat in silence, drinking our coffee. My legs stretched out on his lap. Periodically he rubbed my shin with his strong muscular hands and threw me a killer smile.

"Are you doing okay?" he asked after more silence between us.

I tilted my head and smiled. "I am."

He continued to rub my legs but used both hands with longer strokes. I was melting beneath his touch and couldn't ask him to stop. He started at my ankles. He kneaded my skin with a firm grip as he moved his hands over my shins and the top of my thighs. "You have good muscular legs," he stated. He squeezed my thighs firmly. "All that hiking will keep your legs toned," he added. I didn't know how to react to the compliment. I wasn't used to them. "Yeah, but they are short and stubby. I'm only five foot six. You know."

Travis slapped my thigh and tickled my waist. I winced from his attack and brought my knees up to my chest. "I told you not to tickle me." I protested while giggling.

"Well, stop downing yourself. You're a beautiful woman, and I wish you would see that."

He held my waist with his hands. His grip was firm. "I do." He said while locking his eyes with mine.

Before I could respond, his lips were on mine. I froze. Unsure of what to do. Should I react and kiss him back? I couldn't. I panicked and pushed him away while curling my knees under my chin and cowering back against the couch. "Stop!" I screeched with my eyes wide.

CHAPTER 5

CLAIRE

Travis had every right to feel confused. I'd given him all the signs that I was into him, and then I pushed him away.

"I kissed you because I like you," Travis said with a nervous smile. "And I thought you liked me too."

I ran my hands through my hair. "I do, Travis." I let out a nervous laugh. "It's been a long time. I don't know how to do this anymore."

Travis creased his brow. "What, you've forgotten how to kiss?"

I tossed my head back and realized how stupid I sounded. "No, this." I pointed to him and I. "This whole interacting thing. I can't remember the last time someone touched me. It feels weird. I'm sorry."

Travis gave me a smile that put me at ease. "Come here," he said as he held out his arms.

I unfolded my body and cradled myself in his arms. I rested my face against his lean chest. His hold was powerful, and his massive six-foot frame soothed me. I closed my eyes and felt the warmth of his breath tickle the back of my neck.

He kissed the back of my neck gently. "It's okay, Claire," he whispered.

My neck tingled from his touch, and my heart raced. I breathed short, sharp breaths as I anticipated his next move.

His kisses changed to slow sensual butterfly ones, and I closed my eyes when he swept my hair away from my skin. His touch soft, his lips moist. Every nerve in my body peaked. My heart hammered beneath my chest, and my breaths turned into short elevated pants. The tight hold I had around his waist became looser. I had no more resistance and caved. I knew then that I wanted him.

I've not slept with many men, and the ones I had were not pleasurable experiences. The first was curiosity. Everyone I knew was having sex except me, and I was jealous. It was rough and quick—not a great first-time experience. It left me shattered and ashamed.

Then there was the guy who I thought liked me as much as I liked him. He ended up crushing my heart. It turned out I was just another mark on his scorecard. Since then, I've been afraid to love. I'm so scared to be made a fool of. That was until I met Travis, who I had a hunger for and wanted. Waves of passion and lust swept through me that I had not felt in a long time. Slowly, I will invite him into my world. It seemed we were both unhappy in our lives, and together we brought each other a little bit of happiness.

I raised my head and gazed into his eyes. "Travis, what are we doing?"

With a light feathery touch, he stroked the side of my cheek. "Shh, it's okay."

I nuzzled my face into the palm of his hand and pressed my lips against his skin. "Oh, you smell so good," I whispered before I lifted my head to meet his eyes again. I knew this time; I couldn't resist.

I found myself lost in his gaze—nothing else mattered. It was Travis and me. For the first time, I felt beautiful and desirable. I wanted this moment never to end. My heart was full. I craved more of the heated sensations that raced through my body and the sensitive nerve endings that ignited when Travis touched me—it was mind-blowing.

I sat motionless, facing him. My palms rested on his thighs as he lifted his hands. He removed my glasses and placed them on the table. He returned his gaze to my eyes and cradled my face in his hands. "You are so beautiful, Claire," he whispered. He leaned in and kissed me on my lips.

I closed my eyes and embraced his touch. My mouth remained shut as I kissed him back, but it didn't last long. The warm sensation started at my toes and traveled to my chest. My head became light, and my body weightless. There was no turning back. I hooked my arms around his neck and pulled him closer. I parted my lips to welcome his tongue. When we kissed, it intensified into a hungry, passionate state where we became one.

With our lips still locked, Travis rolled me onto the couch. I sunk into the cushions as he stretched his body over mine and kissed me with more fire as he ground his hips across my thighs. We didn't speak. We didn't need to talk. Neither one of us wanted to fight the heated passion between us. And it was too strong to ignore. Our desire for each other headed into overdrive.

In a passionate frenzy, we panted like overheated dogs. We unlocked our lips for a few seconds to strip away our clothes. Our eyes locked on each other. I tore off my clothes in haste and tossed them to the floor. Travis did the same. For the first time, I wasn't self-conscious about my body. In fact, I felt sexy, and it felt frigging amazing. From the corner of my eye, I saw Tilly scurry off to my bedroom and cracked a laugh. The poor girl had never seen me act this way. Then again, nor have I.

Pumped by a force of adrenaline, I undressed faster than Travis. He stood before me half-naked, and it fixated me as he ripped off his jeans and underwear. Man, he was magnificent in every way. A tight chest and abs that boasted his biceps. I took in a deep breath as he towered over me. His chest heaved. I couldn't hold back and reached out to touch it. His masculine scent overpowered me. I closed my eyes as I took in another deep breath and ran my fingers over his well-defined abs.

"You are in every way," I said while tracing my lips with my tongue.

He lowered his body onto mine, and I drew in short, quick breaths. Our nakedness met at the hips, and then he kissed me hard on the lips. "And you are the most beautiful woman, inside and out," he said in bated breath.

With an urgency to have my body explored by his hands, I moaned and arched my back and guided his head to my naked breasts. Travis glided his tongue over my perky nipples. He caressed my breasts and massaged them with deep strokes. I moaned again, but this time louder and ground my hips against his now erect manhood. Travis kneaded my breasts harder and met my rhythm with his body.

Within seconds our pace had quickened to fast circular motions of our hips and loud heavy breathing. As I continued to release loud drawn-out moans, Travis lowered his mouth onto one of my breasts and sucked it hard. I gasped from his sensual exploration of my body and pulled on his hair. I tugged it again, but with more force when his hand reached between my thighs. I spread my legs slightly. I was ready.

My fire seemed to spark again. Every nerve ending was alive. Never had I felt this way. It drove me fucking crazy. "Travis, I want you. I want you now!" I screamed as I spread my legs wider.

Travis didn't wait for a second longer. He entered me quickly, burying himself deep inside of me with short, hard thrusts. We became one and moaned out loud as we enjoyed the magical sensations that swept through our bodies. I melted like butter and held on to Travis's hips as he rode me hard and fierce. With his hands on my shoulders, I ground against him with my back arched as he increased his pace. As his rhythm quickened, I moaned louder and more frequent. His face turned red. He squeezed his eyes shut, and when he climaxed, he roared and thrusted himself deep inside of me.

I let out a scream after each hard thrust, and after the third one, I yelled his name. "Oh, Travis! I'm going to come!" My body jolted from the sensational orgasm. It was frigging amazing. I reached the highest peak in any orgasm I had ever experienced, and I didn't want it to end. My body convulsed slowly as the orgasm subsided. Travis remained inside me until my body lay limp, and I had finally come back down to earth.

My mind spun with the realization of what we had just done. Everything happened so fast. Once Travis had broken away from me, my body became chilled. I pulled myself up and sat with my back against the cushions and my knees up under my chin. I didn't know what to say, and instead, tears streamed down my face.

"My god, Claire. Are you okay?" Travis said as he scooted his body closer to mine and stroked my sweaty, damp hair out of my face.

I shook my head. I didn't want to be acting this way, but I couldn't help it. We made beautiful love together that I knew was the real deal. I felt the chemistry between us and the uncontrollable desire that put us in what I now found to be an uncomfortable predicament.

I looked up into his worried eyes; tears continued to gush down my cheeks. "Oh Travis, what have we done? I didn't mean for this to happen." I shook my head and wiped my face with the back of my hand. "Not yet, anyway." I felt myself becoming hysterical, and I think Travis saw it too.

He lowered his head to meet my eyes and took me in his arms. "Hey, now. It's okay," he said as he rubbed my shoulders. "Your trembling." He pulled the blanket draped over the couch and covered my shivering body, and rubbed my legs. He looked concerned. "Please don't tell me you have regrets. Neither of us planned this, and I don't want it to scare you away. It shows how much attraction there is between us. I don't think we could have stopped it even if we wanted to."

I took his hand and held it up close to my face. His skin was warm on my cheek. I looked at it for a second and then buried my face in his palm and squeezed his fingers tight. "Oh, Travis. I wasn't expecting this to happen. I thought we had it under control. I know things for you and Jill are over." I needed to repeat myself. "I know that." I kissed his hand again. "I honestly do." I wiped one more time.

Travis listened without interrupting me.

I released a nervous chuckle as I sniffed back my now runny nose. "I've fantasized about us together when I'm alone in my bed, and it's beautiful like tonight was. It was better than my fantasy. I love how you make me feel special and sexy. I want to be with you all the time, Travis." I stopped and choked back more tears and looked at him through my glazed eyes. "I don't want to be the other woman Travis. I can't, and I won't."

I saw the hurt on his face. "Oh, Claire. You won't be. I've told you there's nothing left between Jill and me." He took me in his arms and buried his head in my hair. "I'll make this right, okay."

I lifted my head and kissed him hard on the lips and cradled his face in my hands. I looked deep into his eyes, not breaking my stare. "You're an amazing man, Travis. I don't know what you see in me but thankful that you see something I don't." I let out another subtle laugh. "You've uplifted me in so many ways that I've lost count. With that said—what happened tonight was unexpected, and I don't want anyone to get hurt over this." I kissed him again. "I know we'll be together, and I will count the days, weeks." I took a deep breath. "My concern is Jill. Don't rush home and tell her it's over. I want you two to be adults about it. If you say there is no love left, then sit her down and end it maturely where no one gets hurt and when you know the time is right."

Travis kissed me back and gave me a smile that moved me. "You are one of a kind, Claire. I mean that." He pressed his forehead against mine and spoke more with his eyes staring into mine. "We will be together soon, I promise. I want it to be harmonious when I end it with Jill." He reached down and cupped my chin. He pulled my chin toward his eyes until they were level with his. "Tonight wasn't a mistake, Claire. It just happened sooner than expected."

I didn't break away from his stare. "I know that, Travis. I would never call it a mistake. It was beautiful, but let's refrain from it happening again until we are together."

Travis nodded and smiled. "I agree with you, but I can't lie, it will be tough. I'm okay with it."

"Thank you. I just don't want this to be any more complicated than it already is. I mean shit, I have to work with Jill tomorrow. I hadn't thought about it until now." I shook my head and kept the blanket wrapped around me as I pulled myself off the couch. "I don't want to think about that right now."

Travis looked up from the couch, still naked. His body was hot as hell. "It hadn't crossed my mind either. Are you going to be okay?" he asked.

"Yeah, I'll be fine." I leaned down and tapped his knee. "Listen, I got to pee. I'll be right back."

Travis chuckled while reaching for his t-shirt. "Okay."

When I returned from the bathroom, dressed in my bathrobe, Travis had dressed and was putting on his shoes. I noticed Tilly had returned and curled up in her bed.

I stretched my arms above my head and let out a loud yawn. "What time is it?"

Travis glanced at his phone on the table. "A little after eleven." He looked concerned. "Are you sure you will be okay? He asked. He then added, "Don't hate me, okay."

I gave him a puzzled look as I took a seat next to him and rubbed his thigh. "I don't hate you, silly. Don't start getting all weird on me now." I laughed. "I know we'll get through this and so will Jill."

Travis looked surprised when I mentioned Jill's name.

I rubbed his thigh again as I talked to him. "Neither of us meant for this to happen, but it did. I knew there was some chemistry between us. I just didn't realize how much. It was overpowering for the both of us. Don't you agree?"

"Hell yeah! It was off the charts."

I leaned back and let out a brief chuckle. "Funny thing is I don't feel bad about it or upset about Jill. I know your relationship with Jill is over, and that kind of makes it easier for me to face her at work. But if we continue to have sex until you officially end it with her, well, that would be too weird." I shook my head. "I'm not sure if that makes any sense to you, but it does to me."

Travis nodded and swept his hand across the side of my face. "Yes, it does. You're an amazing woman. I love how you look at everything from a mature aspect." He leaned in and gave me a light peck on the cheek. "As much as I want to stay, I should get going."

"I agree. It's late, and I have to be up at six." I raised my hands to his shoulders and began pushing him off the couch. "Now go on. Get out of here." I said playfully.

Travis laughed. "Okay," he said as he stood to his feet.

I pulled myself off the couch and met him in an embrace. He kissed me gently on my lips. "Can I see you soon?" he asked.

I placed my palms on his chest and patted him. "Sure, but not here." I laughed. "Coffee and dinner yes and more of our in-depth conversations, which I loved. But If you come back here, I know damn well what will happen, and I can't handle that right now." I tilted my head slightly. "It's not fair to us, and even though we had sex tonight, it shouldn't have happened while you are still with Jill."

Travis nodded. "You're right. Give me a little time to talk to her, okay?"

I smiled. I understood he wanted no harsh feelings. "Take all the time you need. I'm not going anywhere." I chuckled before I gave him another shove. "Now go on, get out of here. I need my beauty sleep—Lots of it," I said with a sarcastic laugh.

"Okay, I'm going," he halted at the door. "I just wanted to say that I'd forgotten what it's like to be happy with someone. It's been a long time." He smiled across the room, and I smiled back.

"Well, this is a first for me. I thought I would never meet someone that I could care about." I blew him a kiss. "Good night, Travis."

"Good night, Claire."

And then he left.

CHAPTER 6

TRAVIS

It was hard to say goodnight to Claire. I honestly didn't want to leave. I've never felt so close to someone. Sex with Claire tonight was not planned. When we kissed, I craved more and couldn't hold back. When she kissed me back the second time, her body language told me she felt the same way. It wasn't a friendly peck; it was raw, delicious, and passionate. I knew she felt the same way. Yes, it's fast and unexpected, but it feels so right. I'm not sure if we have a future. Having sex, as we did, may have ruined any chance we had.

Jill and I need to come to terms that our relationship died a long time ago. Both of us have been living in denial for too long. Afraid to admit that it's over. I've been afraid of hurting Jill and moving on. Jill has never been one to talk when we have had problems in the past. She always waited for me to bring it up and fix it, and I did. There was a time when I cared about us, and I would do anything for Jill. I couldn't stand to see her upset, but it got to be one thing after another. I didn't tell her I loved her enough or said she was pretty. She always wanted me to buy her things to prove my love for her and would get upset when I told her I couldn't afford something she wanted.

When our sex life dried up, I became concerned. We used to have sex almost every night, sometimes twice a day. I won't deny it. We were hot together. Then it dwindled to once a week. At the time, I blamed it on work. I was working long hours and was in bed by ten. Jill stayed up to watch her nightly TV shows. Sex once a week soon turned into a few times a month, and when we did, it felt forced. Almost like a chore. And now it's been months. The last time I bought sex up, it turned into an argument. Not quite the turn-on I was looking for. It was about three months before I met Claire. We hadn't had sex in weeks. I was sitting on the couch, watching TV, and she had just come downstairs after taking a bath. I tried to make her feel good and complimented her.

"You smell good. How was your bath?" I said as she approached the coffee table dressed in a pink silk nightgown that stopped halfway up her thighs. She didn't look at me and grabbed her phone.

"It was better than lazing around on the couch." She snapped. Her eyes glued to the screen of her phone.

Her reply hit a nerve. "What's that supposed to mean?"

She tapped away on her phone when she answered. "It means I got bored, so I took a bath. Every night you sit on the damn couch and watch TV. You never pay attention to me."

I rolled my eyes. "Jill, the other night, I tried to kiss you, and you pushed me away. You said my breath stank and went upstairs. I've tried to get close to you, and you just won't let me."

"Don't blame me because you can't get it up anymore. I'm not going to have sex with you when you stink. You could at least take a shower when you come home."

"Since when has that fucking bothered you. We used to fuck our brains out morning, noon, and night. I never remember you saying—hey, can you take a shower first?" I shook my head. "Give me a break. You're always making excuses, and I'm tired of being rejected. Suddenly, I'm not good enough for you."

"There you go blaming me again. It isn't my fault, Travis. I don't need this shit. I'm going to bed."

"Fine!" I snapped, and if I had the beginnings of a hard-on, it had disappeared in a flash.

I didn't know what to do. Everything I said sparked anger in her, and we didn't talk about sex again.

Jill's solution to our problems was to walk around with a chip on her shoulder, slam doors, and be damn right mean. She doesn't talk to me; she snaps at me about everything.

I don't think it will surprise her when I confront her. I have a feeling she will be relieved. I think the only reason we're still together is that neither one of us wanted to admit it first. Yeah, I'm a little sad that what we once had is no more. We were great in the beginning, and it's hard to believe that there is nothing left. It will take a few days for me to get my thoughts together. Then I'm going to sit her down and tell her it's over.

But it wasn't that easy. Over the past few weeks, Jill and I had become estranged but still lived under the same roof. Most mornings, I was up at five and left by seven. Jill would avoid me by staying in bed. After work, I was in no rush to go home and stopped at a restaurant and ate alone or met up with Claire. Other nights I hung out with Slater and Sabela.

There had been many nights that Jill didn't come home until close to midnight. She never called to let me know her plans. We never called each other anymore. We were only together for an hour at a time, a few days a week, and we had nothing to say to each other anymore. You could cut the tension between us with a knife, and I tried to avoid it as much as possible. When she was home, she slammed doors, stormed around the condo cursing under her breath, and to avoid talking to me, texted me on her phone. When she looked at me, she reflected only hatred. If she hates me so much, why is she still with me? Why hasn't she ended it?

Since our night of unexpected passion, Claire and I had met for dinner once a week. The rest of the time, she had been on my mind often. When I did see her, it took all of my willpower not to take her in my arms and kiss her intensively. But I never could. Man, it was tough to keep my hands to myself.

During a moment of weakness, I caved in and told Slater about my failed relationship with Jill and that I started seeing someone. I had to tell someone; it drove me crazy. I went against my better judgment and was selfish when I shared details of my crazy world with him, but I couldn't stand it anymore–it just came out. I regretted it the minute I told him, but it was too late, I couldn't take it back. I had spoken before I had thought it through.

A few days later, I met Claire for dinner. When she sat down at the table across from me, she didn't greet me with her cute, sexy smile that made my heart go pitter-patter. She looked sad, and it worried me.

Her swollen eyes told me she had been crying. "Hey, are you okay?" I asked. I took her hand across the table where we sat.

She shook her head and buried her head in her hands.

"Claire. What's going on?" I gave her hand a gentle squeeze. She pulled it away and rested her hands in her lap.

It scared me. "Claire, you're scaring me. Talk to me."

She raised her head and reached for a napkin. I waited while she wiped her eyes.

"Claire?" I asked again.

"Oh, Travis. I can't do this anymore."

I frowned. "Do what?"

"This. Us. All this secret stuff. It's not right." Tears flowed down her cheeks again. "I want to be with you. I want to go to bed with you at night and fall asleep in your arms. I want to wake up with you in the morning and sit and have coffee with you." She sniffed to hold back her tears and choked out her next words. "I want to have sex with you and not my frigging vibrator."

"I want all of that too, Claire."

She looked at me and spoke with a sharp tone, One I had not

heard before. "Then do something about it. We can't go on like this." She raised her hands slightly along with her voice. "I can't go on like this. Every day I see Jill and listen to her bitch about you," Claire grunted. "I just want to slap her." She folded her arms across her chest and leaned back. "You know what she said to me yesterday?"

"No, what?"

"She said if she had another guy lined up, she'd leave you in a heartbeat." Claire's temper rose.

She had enough of our arrangement, so I can't say I blame her. I'd had enough too, especially when I see Claire so upset and angry.

"Why the hell are you two still living together. It's been almost a month since you told me you would end it with Jill. I can't keep this to myself much longer." Claire held up her hand and pinched her thumb and index finger together. "Do you want to know something? I came this close to telling her about us earlier this week," Claire hissed.

Her confession shocked me. "What? Why? What happened?"

"Earlier this week before office hours, she came into the break room just heaving and stomping her feet, yelling how she hates men. I was at the coffee machine and tried to ignore her, but I was the only one in the room, so that was impossible." Claire took a breath and shook her head. "She started yelling at me, Travis. I don't need this shit."

"What did she say," I asked.

"Her exact words were. *You're so lucky you don't have to deal with men. Keep it that way. You've never had a boyfriend, have you, Claire?*" Claire rolled her fist." I wanted to punch her right there. Where does she come off insulting me like that? She knows nothing about me. It was then I thought about telling her about you and me, but I bit my tongue, gave her the evil eye and said, *It's none of your business. And for your information, not that it's any of your business, I have had a boyfriend, Jill.*" And then I stormed out of the room. Claire let out an angry grunt. "I'm sick of this whole situation, Travis."

I reached across the table for her hand, but she pulled away. "I'm sorry. It is all wrong. It's not fair to you. But thanks for not saying anything. It's my job, not yours."

Claire leaned back with a look of despair. "I know I said for you to take your time. But damn it, Travis, I have feelings too." She shook her head and took a sip of wine that the waiter had just set down. "I know you don't want to upset Jill, but after what she told me yesterday, trust me, she'll be relieved that one of you has finally ended it."

"I'm sorry. I don't enjoy seeing you upset. It's all my fault. I should have told Jill weeks ago. She's so damn angry, and it's hard to have a civil conversation when she gets like that."

Claire slammed her hands on the table. I glanced around to see if anyone heard the loud bang. A couple across from us did, and I avoided their stares.

Claire's eyes narrowed as she spoke in a harsh whisper. "Quit making excuses, Travis. I'm sorry, but I can't do this anymore. Go home and tell Jill and then call me so we can get on with our lives." She picked up a napkin and dabbed her brow and then removed her glasses and wiped them with force as she spoke. "I don't know why you and Jill have such a problem telling each other it's over." She cracked a laugh. "She wishes she had another guy lined up for god sakes." Claire couldn't hide her frustrations. Her tone became sharp, and her eyes narrowed. She leaned back and folded her arms. "Tell me, Travis. Is there still some love left between you and Jill? Is that why you are having a hard time moving on?" She curled her lip and snarled at me. "I was made a fool of too many times before. I won't let it happen again."

She had every right to be angry, but her last comment shocked me. "Now wait a minute, Claire. I will never make a fool out of you." I scanned the tables around us and lowered my voice. "I've had enough too. I can't keep this bottled up inside anymore. It's driving me fucking crazy." I rolled my eyes. "Just the other day, I told Slater that Jill and I aren't getting along and that I was seeing someone."

"You didn't!" Claire gasped. Her eyes were twice their normal size. "Are you insane? Why would you do that?" She shook her head in disbelief. "Sabela and Jill are close friends, and you don't think she's going to say something to her?"

I hovered my hands over the table. "Now calm down. I asked Slater not to say anything, and I believe him. Look, I'm telling Jill tonight. I don't care what happens. I can handle it, but what I won't be able to handle is you hating me too."

Claire went silent for a minute and nodded. "Okay, then. I'm happy to hear it."

When I saw Claire upset and angry, I realized just how stupid and selfish I'd been. Now I couldn't wait to come clean and move on. "Can we not talk about this anymore and enjoy our meal? Afterward, I'm going straight home to take care of everything once and for all."

Claire threw me a smile and picked up her menu. "Sure," she said before browsing her choices of meals.

Our moods had improved over dinner, or so I thought. "I can't wait until I can kiss you," I whispered after we had finished our meal.

Claire gave me a piercing stare. "Well, you know what to do."

I sensed she was still upset. "Are you still mad?" I asked.

She avoided my eyes. "I've tried to be happy through it all, but it's difficult when I know you'll be going home to her and not with me."

"I promise this will be the last time. I'm leaving tonight," I said with an edge to my voice.

Her sadness returned. "I hope so, Travis." She shook her head and threw her napkin in haste onto the table. "I'm going to the restroom."

"Wait, Claire," I begged.

She shook her head. "Travis, I've been waiting." She rose to her feet.

It was then that I saw tears pooled in her eyes. It crushed my heart. "Claire, let's talk some more."

She gave her head a hard shake. "No! I need a minute," she said before she stormed off.

I refused to wait at the table alone. I feared she might not come back and raced to the restrooms, where I waited outside the door of the women's bathroom. I nodded at the women who entered and gave me strange looks as they walked by. *What if she went straight home and bypassed the bathroom altogether? Should I ask someone if she is in there?* I paced back and forth and wondered what to do. *Please, Claire, come on out. Please be there.* I didn't know how long I waited, but it felt like an eternity. Every time the door swung open, I held my breath, hoping it was Claire. It sank when it was not.

I had just about given up and was about to return to the table to settle the dinner check when the door swung open again. I froze and stared hard at the door. Claire stood before me and had been crying. Her eyes were red, her cheeks flushed.

I rushed to her side, "Claire, I'm sorry."

She dabbed her swollen eyes with the paper towel that she had scrunched in her hand. "I hate this, Travis. I hate going home alone."

I placed my hands on her shoulders and leveled my eyes with hers. "I know, and I will be with you soon."

"Will you? I don't know anymore."

I had to stop her from saying something she might regret, and with force, I kissed her hard on the lips and used my strength to guide her back to the nearby wall. Once I had her with her back pressed against the wall, she broke away and pressed her palms firmly on my chest.

"Travis, what are you doing?"

I kissed her again. But it had more force behind it than the first.

I leaned in and pushed up against her body, pinning her to the wall. "I'm kissing you, that's what I'm doing."

Claire tried to turn her head away, but I was stronger." Travis, we can't." She muffled with my lips pressed on hers."

"Yes, we can, and we are. Tell me; you will see me tomorrow when I am a free man."

I felt her body loosen. She was no longer rigid. I softened my kiss, and her hands eased away from my chest and up around my neck. I found her tongue and devoured her taste. Our kiss lingered and left me breathless. "Will I see you tomorrow.?"

She broke a small smile and gave me a nod. "Yes, you will see me tomorrow."

I released a sigh of relief and patted my heart." Oh, Claire, you had me so scared. Don't give up on us, okay?. We're so close. Please don't throw it all away."

"Just do something okay. I'm going to go home."

I held her face in my hand and kissed her one more time. "I will."

~

I returned to the place I had called home for the last four years. Come to think of it, I hadn't thought past tonight, and what my plans would be after I had told Jill we were through. Thoughts raced through my mind. I hoped to have a place to sleep after tonight. I didn't know where I would be staying tomorrow. I doubt I'd be staying here.

I pulled into my parking space next to Jill's pink mustang and turned off the motor. I sat for a few moments and enjoyed the silence. I needed to brace myself for the storm that lay ahead. As I stepped out of the truck, I noticed most of the lights were on in the condo, which I assumed meant Jill was still up. *Better than waking her.* I thought.

Once inside, Jill was nowhere in sight. I heard the bathtub

draining upstairs. Her usual routine, if I was home, was to go straight to bed. I wouldn't allow that to happen tonight and darted up to the bathroom and knocked on the door.

"What?" Jill hollered in a harsh tone from the other side.

"We need to talk. Meet me downstairs when you're done."

I pictured her rolling her eyes. "Can't it wait?" She said, using the same tone.

"No, it can't. Come down here, please."

"Fine," she snapped.

I didn't respond and went to get some liquid courage from the fridge. After popping open a beer, I sat at the kitchen table and took a huge gulp. I smacked my lips from the satisfying taste and waited for Jill. I scanned the room and felt a slight twinge of sadness because I knew I would never come back, but with that said, I had no second thoughts or doubts. I'd dragged this out too long, which resulted in Claire getting upset. Tomorrow was going to be the first day of my new life, and I couldn't wait to get it started. The only thing I was afraid of was Jill's reaction. It was because of her that my palms were clammy, and beads of sweat formed on my brow.

After ten minutes and a second beer, I heard Jill's footsteps descending down the stairs. I shifted in my seat and wiped my brow. She wore a pink bathrobe and matching furry slippers. "What's all this about?" she asked when she approached the table with her hands on her hips.

I shifted again in my chair. "Have a seat."

She rolled her eyes. "You know, I'm exhausted. Can you make this quick?" She pulled out a chair and sat across from me. She folded her arms and gave me a piercing stare; it didn't intimidate me. It was the only stare she gave me nowadays.

I took a large gulp of beer. "Are you happy, Jill?" I asked.

She leaned back in her chair, keeping her arms folded. Her lips curled as she spoke, and her eyes narrowed even more. "No. Can't you tell?"

"So tell me. Jill, why are we still together? We haven't been getting along for months."

Jill's mouth lowered. "Is there something I've done wrong?"

I released a sarcastic laugh. "Oh come on, Jill, don't act so surprised. We've been going through this for months. I think we've taken this relationship as far as it can go."

"So, what are you saying?"

I shook my head and tilted it back. "Do I have to spell it out for you?"

"Are you saying we should break up?"

I didn't hesitate with my answer and came right out and said it. "Yes, I do. I don't want to live like this anymore, Jill." I paused. "Do you?"

After I said what should have been said months ago, I sucked in some air and exhaled deeply. I wasn't upset; it relieved me. I looked at Jill. She hadn't shed a tear or disagreed with me about anything. There were no tears between us. I finally said what needed to be said, and it felt like I had lifted an enormous weight off my shoulders.

She remained silent.

"Don't you agree?" I asked again.

She nodded, unfolded her arms, and crossed her hands in her lap, "Yeah, I guess. But I want to know why you don't enjoy being around me?"

I shook my head. "Why does it matter? I don't even know I could ask you the same thing. You avoid me like the plague. Why does everything have to be about you?"

"It doesn't," she snapped.

"Yes, it does." I raised my hands in defeat. She doesn't get it. In disgust, I left the table to grab another beer. "You always complain that I do nothing for you." I hollered from the kitchen and yanked the fridge door open.

"Well, you don't." She squealed like a spoiled child.

I looked across the room at her and narrowed my eyes. "Really?

All the clothes, the membership to your gym, the jewelry, and let's not forget who paid all the damn bills here. I shook my head. Unbelievable Jill. I don't buy you anything? See how it's all about what I'm not doing for you. Tell me, what have you ever done for me?" I turned to face the fridge in search of a much needed third beer. "See you don't have an answer, do you?" I snarled as I reached inside the fridge and grabbed the last beer.

"I've done things for you?" Jill contested.

I returned to the table and slid into a chair before I popped open the beer and took a big swig. "Really? Name something?"

It was Jill's turn to shift in her seat. She raised her tone a notch. "I can't think right now. Stop asking me stupid questions."

I released a sarcastic laugh. "That's because there isn't anything. It's over, Jill. Let's face it. We had a great ride, but we have nothing left to give."

She folded her arms again. "So, what happens now?"

"I'll come and get my stuff tomorrow, and I'll leave the key on the counter."

Jill leaned back in her chair and gritted her teeth. "So you're leaving tonight? You don't waste any time, do you?"

I laughed at her remark. "Ha! What's there to stick around for? So we can have more conversations like this. We've procrastinated getting to this point for months. Why drag it out any longer?"

"Fine." She hissed. "But let me ask you something. Have you been seeing someone else?"

Her question took me by surprise. I thought we would leave on good terms. We both understood that our relationship was over, and we had accepted it. It surprised me how well she took it, and how calm she acted. Maybe she's relieved as I am. But it could change matters drastically, and I couldn't lie to her. She'd find out, eventually. But it was over before I started seeing Claire. I shrugged my shoulders. "Well, sort of."

Her eyes cut me like a knife, and her body became rigid. Hatred was all I saw. "Sort of? What's that supposed to mean? Either you are, or you're not? Which is it, Travis?" she yelled before slamming her palms on the table.

I didn't like where this was going, Jill had a temper, and I feared it might explode. "She's a friend. We've had dinner a few times."

"Have you slept with her," Jill asked. Her nostrils flared.

I took another large swig of my beer. "Once okay. That's all. It just happened, and nothing has happened since."

Jill stood up and pushed her chair to the ground with the back of her knees. She paced the kitchen floor, "And that's supposed to make it okay?" she snarled.

"No, but you asked, and I'm being honest, okay."

"Do I know her?" She raised her hands and cupped her head. "Never mind. I don't want to know. Just go." she yelled while waving me away.

I didn't want to pursue this anymore. What was the point? I did what I needed to do, and Jill agreed that we should break up. She showed no anger until she found out I was seeing someone. Even if I wasn't, our break-up was bound to happen eventually. "Look, I'm sorry. I'll come by tomorrow and get my stuff."

She didn't look at me. Instead, she tugged at her robe and headed up the stairs. "Just go," she yelled without looking back.

I chugged down my beer and left the empty bottle on the table, and headed out the door to begin my search for a hotel room.

CHAPTER 7

CLAIRE

When I woke up Saturday morning, Travis entered my mind. I stayed up late last night expecting to hear from him, but he never called. He left the restaurant eager to go home and end it with Jill. I wondered if he did? Disappointment hung over me. I sat down on the edge of the bed and waited for that expected phone call.

Even though I didn't go to bed until after midnight, I woke up at my usual time of 7:00 to wet kisses smothering my face. "Okay, Tilly. I'm up." I squealed as she licked my face. "I'll take you out in a minute."

Tilly barked with approval; she had done her job. I was awake. She barked again and jumped off the bed. She disappeared into the front room.

I stretched and left the comfort of my bed to make some coffee. My day doesn't begin until after I've had that first cup. Once the machine made its familiar gurgling sound, I breathed in the heavy scent of the coffee brewing. I inhaled the aroma of the coffee, and my body came alive.

I had hoped Travis left me a message, so I grabbed my phone

from the bedroom nightstand. I picked it up, held my breath, and glanced at the screen: nothing, not a single word. I lounged on the bed, the palms of my hands covered in sweat. My heart dropped into my stomach. "Damn it, Travis. Will you call me and let me know what the hell is going on?" I yelled and stormed off to the kitchen. Tilly pawed my knees and barked. A reminder that I needed to take her outside. I reached down and petted her head. "Okay, Tilly, you win. But I'm not going out in my PJs." I told her. I headed back into the bedroom and grabbed my bathrobe hanging on the back of the door.

I stood in the cold for ten minutes. When Tilly finished her business, I scooped her up and headed to the condo. After I closed the door, I heard the familiar ding sound of a text message from my phone and quickly put Tilly down. She barked at a dog on the TV. No matter what show is on, if a dog appears on the screen, Tilly goes into attack mode. "Tilly, it's just the TV. Hush!" I said as I hunted for my phone, forgetting where I had left it," Tilly ignores me. "Tilly! Hush!" I repeated it, this time in a louder and firmer tone. Finally, she listened and retreated to her bed. "Good girl. Now, where the hell did I put my phone?" It dinged again. I followed the sound to the kitchen and breathed in the powerful aroma of coffee that invaded the room. I scanned the area and found the phone on the counter next to the coffee pot.

There's a text from Travis.

It's done, call me.

My eyes grew wide. "Wow! He did it," I yelled. I needed coffee before I called him back.

I was eager to hear how it went, but I needed fueling by my coffee first. With the hot beverage in one hand and my cellphone in the other, I headed over to the couch to enjoy my morning ritual of the morning news and coffee. But it didn't last long. I had a lot of questions for Travis and wondered how he was doing. If he had told Jill last night, then where did he stay? I muted the TV and called him.

After two rings, he answered. He sounded tired. "Hey, Claire. Did you get my text? I told Jill."

"I did. I was outside with Tilly and left my phone inside. So how did it go?"

"She agreed with everything I had to say and didn't argue when I said we should split up. We were being civil to one another and having an adult conversation about everything until I blew it."

"You blew it? What do you mean?" I asked, feeling a sudden sense of uneasiness.

"I told her I was dating someone else, and then the shit hit the fan."

I gasped. "You didn't." I stood up and paced the room. "Did you tell her it was me? Please say you didn't? I have to work with her, remember." I panicked. I couldn't face Jill, at least not yet.

"No. No, I didn't. Calm down. But I thought she had a right to know I was seeing someone." He paused for a moment. "You do realize she will find out about us? We have to deal with it at some point."

My heart returned to normal as soon as I found out Jill didn't know about me. "Yes, I know that. But I prefer later than sooner so I can prepare myself. So where are you? Did you just now tell her?"

"No, I told her last night. It was late. I didn't want to call you in case you were sleeping, so I got a hotel room."

It disappointed me that he didn't call. "Travis! You didn't have to do that; you could have come here. I wouldn't have minded if you had woken me. Gosh, now I feel bad."

"It's fine. I would not have been the best company. I couldn't sleep anyway, so I would have kept you awake."

"I wouldn't mind that either." I chuckled. "So, what happens now?"

Travis released a nervous cough. "I'm not sure. Jill wants all my stuff out of there this morning. She told me she wouldn't be there. I don't have a lot of things, maybe a few tools, and my clothes. Mainly my tools and stuff. She can keep all the furniture. I need to get this over with. I'm heading over there after I check out. Can I come to your place when I'm finished?"

"Of course. I'm going to get dressed and take Tilly for a walk, and then I'll be home waiting for you."

"Okay. I'm not sure how long this will take. Probably a few hours. I have to swing by Slater's and grab my check."

At the mention of Slater's name, I slipped into panic mode. "You aren't going to tell him about me, are you?"

"No, I'm not. But he and Sabela will find out like Jill, so brace yourself." He said with a slight chuckle.

"Yeah, I know. Okay, I'll see you when you get here."

I hung up the phone. I shuddered at the thought of our relationship being revealed. How would our friends react? Would I suddenly lose three friends because I found someone who I care about and can connect with? The thought sent shivers down my spine. I just wanted to be happy, but it's complicated.? I shook my head, not wanting to think about the what-ifs any more, and went to the bedroom to get dressed.

I didn't hear from Travis until later in the afternoon when he called my cell. When I saw his name flash on my screen, a surge of relief ran through me. I had been on edge all day, anticipating his call. Afraid Jill had made it difficult for him.

"Hey, I'm all done. I got tied up at Slater's place. Can I come over?"

I immediately sensed the happier tone in his voice. He no longer sounded stressed.

"Sure. I've been worried about you. Are you okay?" I asked.

"Yeah, I'm fine. I got all my stuff in my truck. I'll be there soon."

"Okay. I can't wait to see you. Bye."

As I hung up, I lifted Tilly off my lap and put her on the couch cushion next to me so I could check myself in the mirror. Something I rarely did. I stared at my reflection and gave myself a satisfactory smile. For the first time in a while, I liked what I saw. Travis is the first guy I've known that likes me for who I am. I don't have to pretend to be anyone else. I gave my hair a quick brush and applied some lip-gloss. I had contemplated changing my clothes, but I felt comfortable in my jeans and a white checkered shirt and decided against it.

I glanced at my watch and saw it was almost seven and wondered if Travis had eaten dinner yet. I wandered into the kitchen and checked the cupboards. I had a few canned goods and a loaf of bread—the fridge wasn't any better. "Well, I guess it's pizza for dinner," I announced out loud.

Twenty minutes later he knocked at my door, Tilly did her usual door patrol and barked excessively, not giving me any room to open the door. "Hush Tilly," I said in a sharp tone, but it does no good. I finally picked her up and held her in my arms while I opened the door.

On the other side, I find Travis leaning against the wall. His eyes were heavy, and his body was limp. "Hey. You look beat. Come on in," I said as I rubbed his arm.

He threw me a smile and pulled himself away from the wall. "I am," he said as he leaned in and gave me an unexpected kiss.

It was a slow, tender kiss that lingered and made my toes curl. I closed my eyes and enjoyed the warmth of his lips, touching mine. "I smell beer," I whispered.

He broke away and chuckled. "Yeah, I had a few with Slater. I needed them after today."

"Come on in," I said. I sat Tilly on the floor, who immediately barked again. "Tilly, no!"

Travis laughed at her excessive barking and leaned down to pet her. "It's okay, girl," he said in a soft, calm voice as he stroked her back.

Tilly enjoyed her moment of attention and showed her appreciation with a constant licking of Travis's hand. I led him over to the couch, where we made ourselves comfortable. Tilly had to join us and jumped on Travis's lap as soon as he sat down.

"Well, I guess you made a new friend," I laughed. "Did you eat?"

Travis shook his head. "Nah. I'm not hungry."

"I rubbed his thigh as we spoke. What do Sabela and Slater think about you and Jill splitting up? I know Sabela is close to Jill. Do you think they blame you for everything?"

"I think they did at first, but after I had explained to them where my relationship was with her, they understood better." He paused, lowered his eyes to the floor, and avoided my stare. "But..."

My stomach churned, and my heart skipped a beat. I had a feeling of what he was going to say next would not be good. I took a deep breath. "But what?" I asked with a hint of uncertainty.

"I told them about you."

My eyes grew wide, and I gasped. "No! You didn't." Shockwaves jolted through my body. I buried my head in my hands with disbelief. "Why would you do such a thing?"

"Because it needed to be said. They knew I was seeing someone. I can't keep secrets from them if I'm going to be working for them, and they recently gave me a great job opportunity."

"And what was Sabela's reaction?" I snarled and still upset that he had told them.

"At first they were angry, but after I explained to them what an amazing woman you are." He smiled and squeezed my knee. "And how much I care for you, they finally understood and accepted the fact that you are now my girlfriend."

I felt my cheeks blush and gave him a warm smile. "Really?" I held my hand to my chest. "I'm shocked. We never spoke much when we worked together."

Travis laughed. "Well, she wishes us well and even surprised me by suggesting we have dinner at their place sometimes."

I gasped again and raised my voice a notch. "What! Oh, I don't know about that, Travis. My brother tried to rape Sabela. How would she be able to even look at me? And then there's Jill. She's still friends with Jill, right?"

My hands trembled as I chewed on my thumbnail and anticipated a meeting with Slater and Sabela. I didn't know if I could do it. My body rocked with worry, and Travis sensed I was about to go into a full-blown panic mode and pulled me into his space and held me tight. I remained curled in his arms, feeling the tension subside as he rubbed my shoulders.

"Hey, now. We're not talking about that anytime soon. And as far as we know, she might not even follow through. We all agreed to let the dust settle and adjust to the changes." He kissed the top of my head. "And enough about Jill, okay. She's going to be fine, and eventually, she will find out about us, but in the meantime, let's not worry about something that hasn't happened yet, okay"

He was right. I lifted my neck to meet his gaze and smiled. "Okay," I whispered.

"That's better." He said before he leaned in and gave me a tender kiss.

It felt good to be in his arms. I felt protected. I knew this was where I wanted to be. We would get through the reactions of others about our new blossoming relationship, and I hoped eventually everyone would accept us as a couple. I pulled Travis in closer, feeling grateful he was a part of my life and kissed him harder, as I explored the inside of his mouth with my tongue.

Travis gasped a few quick breaths between his words. "I'm sorry it took me so long to do the right thing. But it's just you and me now, babe." He pulled away, leaving me breathless, and cupped my face in his hands. He looked at me with sparkling eyes. "I want to make you happy if you will let me," he said, followed by a sweet loving smile.

"I smiled back and stroked his hand that rested on my face. Only if you let me make you happy too," tears welled up in my eyes.

He continued to look at me with loving eyes that melted my heart when he raked my hair with his fingers. I closed my eyes from his sensual touch. "Just being here with you makes me happy. The rest will fall into place. I promise. Just give it some time." He paused and stroked his hand through my hair again. "Just don't give up on us, okay?" he pleaded.

I squeezed his hand and pulled it down to my lips and kissed his skin gently. "I'll never give up on us. You came into my life so unexpectedly and suddenly and have made my life so much richer in the brief time I have known you." I gave him a cheeky grin. "Now, why would I want to go back to the lonely life I was living before I met you?"

Travis cocked his head back and laughed, "Oh, I love how you make me laugh. I've not laughed in a long time." He pulled me in again. "I can't get enough of you. Being away from you was torture. Come here and give me another kiss." He kissed me hard and afterward beamed a huge smile. "We are together at last."

I gazed into his eyes. "Yes, we are."

Our lips remained glued until Tilly had enough of being ignored and jumped into our laps as she overpowered us with her high-pitched bark. We couldn't help but laugh and together gave her the attention she was seeking.

As we sat together with our foreheads bowed down and looking at Tilly, a thought crossed my mind. "Hey, where will you stay?" I asked. I already knew the answer but wanted to tease Travis a little.

Travis stopped stroking Tilly and leaned back on the couch. "I don't know yet. I haven't given it much thought, I just wanted to get my stuff out, and that's as far as I've gotten."

I rested my hand on his thigh and beamed him a smile. "I know where you can stay."

I sensed Travis knew what I was thinking by his matching grin. "You do?"

"I do." I smiled again and patted his thigh. "You can move in with me."

CHAPTER 8

TRAVIS

I hoped Claire would have asked me to move in with her, but I refused to put her on the spot. I wasn't sure if she was ready to have me crowd her space. Living together could be a huge change for her. My only other option would have been to ask Sabela and Slater if I could crash at their place for a few nights. I'm sure glad it didn't come to that.

I took Claire's hand and stroked her palm with the tips of my fingers. "Are you sure about this? You would be taking a giant leap of faith with me."

She threw me a cute grin and tilted her head slightly. "I've never been so sure about anything in my life. I won't lie; it will take time getting used ti living with someone." She gave me a candid smile. "I have a confession. I've never lived with anyone before."

"You're kidding?" I said with wide eyes. I was shocked by her confession.

Claire shook her head. "Nope, I'm not kidding. It's all new to me. I've told you before I've not dated much, and I haven't found someone I want to share my life with." She squeezed my hand. "Until I met you, that is."

I ran my hand through my hair and pulled it away from my forehead. "Wow. I'm flattered. Well, you won't regret it. I promise I'll be a good roommate."

Claire leaned in closer, causing Tilly to jump off the couch and return to her bed. "You better be more than just a roommate, mister," she laughed and gave me a peck on the cheek.

I pulled her in close and wrapped my arms around her waist. "Oh, I will be so much more," I whispered.

Our eyes met, and for a few seconds, there was a comfortable silence between us. "You are so beautiful. Inside and out, Claire. You're amazing." I gazed into her eyes and gently removed her glasses and set them on the coffee table. "You honestly take my breath away," I whispered. I traced both sides of her face delicately with my fingers. Claire sat still and closed her eyes. Her skin soft, and she smiled when I brushed her lips. "Your lips are perfect. I want to kiss them all the time." I leaned in and touched them with mine. She took a deep breath through her nose and parted her lips to welcome me. I didn't hesitate and invaded her mouth with my tongue. She tasted sweet. In no time, we smothered each other in a deep kiss.

"Claire, I promise to make you a happy woman." I panted between breaths.

"You already do," she said in matching breaths as she pressed her body firmly against mine. She had me pinned to the corner of the couch. I sank back into the cushions, and without letting go of her lips, I pulled her on top of me. She straddled me with her legs bent at the knees and pressed her palms onto my chest before breaking away. I stared at her and placed my hands on her hips. My breaths escalated to short pants, and my heart pounded beneath my chest. My eyes never left hers as I watched with anticipation, undress. She held her back straight as she reached for the sky and smiled. I moistened my lips and grinned as I anxiously waited for her next move. She threw me a cute, sexy smirk, and in a slow provocative move, she pulled off her shirt over her head and gave her hair a good, flirtatious shake. My eyes darted down to her heaving chest, concealed only by a black lace bra. Her breasts, hard and supple-nipples raised and alert.

I reached up and cupped each breast. My hand squeezed them gently. "God, you are magnificent," I told her, memorized by her beauty.

Claire covered her hands with mine and pressed down. She arched her back and moaned as we massaged her breasts together. "Squeeze them hard," she whispered.

The softness of her skin aroused me, and my chest heaved. My body came alive with a sexual urge that I had not experienced in some time. Excited by Claire's touch, I pressed my face deep into her crevice and followed the top of her lace bra with my tongue.

Claire released a satisfying moan and closed her eyes, "oh, yes." She bit her bottom lip and arched her back.

I wasted no time and continued to trace her erect nipples through the black lace with my tongue. I took my time and worked slowly. I wanted to savor the moment and taste every delicious inch of her. I ran my fingers over the edge of her bra and pulled the material away from her skin. She moaned in excitement. I looked at her and smiled. Her breasts were tight, her skin soft, and her sweet perfume engulfed me.

I welcomed the adrenaline rush that raced through my body, fueled by the beautiful woman before me. She was perfect in every way. My sex drive, which had laid dormant for months, had recharged with no hesitation, I kicked it into high gear. Powered by a fierce passion, I yanked her bra down and freed her breasts from the confinement of the bra. Claire moaned and flipped back her head as she buried my face into her chest.

I closed my eyes and inhaled her sweet scent. My heart skipped a few beats as I craved for more. I glided my tongue over her delicate skin and continued to devour her. My mouth switched between each beautiful breast. I was on fire and didn't want it to end anytime soon. I inhaled deep breaths to calm down my racing heartbeat. In a heated frenzy and a tidal wave of lust, I unsnapped her bra and tossed it aside.

I pulled away with a heaving chest and glided my hands over her clean skin. I spread my palms wide and covered every inch of her neck, chest, and stomach, kneading her skin softly with slow circular motions. Claire closed her eyes and held her head back. She shadowed the movement of my hands with hers. She moaned louder and breathed heavier.

I leaned in and kissed her stomach with short butterfly kisses before I circled her belly button with my tongue. "I want you," I whispered softly with bated breath.

Aroused by my confession, Claire gyrated her hips across my lap and pressed down hard on my prominent bulge. She leaned in and met my stare. Her eyes glazed with passion. Her lips were moist. "I want you too," she whispered as she pressed her body hard into my groin.

Our lips met again, but this time with more hunger and force. Her hair whipped across my face. She thrust her hips against me. We locked ourselves in a passionate kiss, our tongues entwined, I reached behind her and pulled her sweat pants down over her thighs. They were loose and slid down easily. Claire aided me in my attempt with a cute, sexy wiggle that fired up my juices even more. I was ready to burst, and with lightning speed, peeled off her panties.

My chest heaved, and I wasn't sure how much longer I could refrain from coming. I brushed her inner thighs with my hand so I could adjust my aching erection. Claire gasped and pressed my hand firmly onto her skin. I shifted my body and motioned for her to stand up. "Come on. I want to see all of you spread out on the bed." I panted as my heart continued to race.

Claire smiled and pulled herself off my lap and rose to her feet. My erection bulges prominently beneath my jeans. Claire's eyes zoned in. She smiled, took my hand, and pulled me up off the couch. She gave my groin a deep, hard rub. "I want this," she whispered into my ear before she nibbled my lobe.

I couldn't wait any longer and took her hand. "Come on," I said.

In haste, we raced to the bedroom. "Lay down and spread your leg," I demanded. "I'm going to be inside of you within the next thirty seconds."

Claire crawled on her knees to the middle of the bed. I watched with a hard-on that wouldn't quit as she wiggled her beautiful ass in the air and giggled. I laughed at the way she teased me and felt like I was the luckiest man in the world. Damn, she looked beautiful, and she was all mine.

"Turn over," I commanded her. "And lay in the center of the bed."

She did as I asked and gave me a sexy laugh before she reached down between her legs and aroused herself with her fingertips.

I wrestled with my belt buckle, unable to take my eyes off the beauty before me. "Oh man, for someone that's not dated much, you sure know how to turn a guy on," I told her as I continued to undress.

She giggled again and tossed her head from side to side before spreading her leg a little further and pleasing herself with her fingers. "Some things you just have to take care of on your own." She laughed.

I struggled with my jeans as I watched her play with herself. My heart raced, and I could feel the sweat bead up on my brow. I could not remember the last time I had been so turned on by a woman. "God, you are so frigging hot." I panted as I balanced on each leg to pull off my jeans.

Claire tasted herself on her finger and grinned. "I have a confession," she whispered.

Naked, I crawled on to the bed and straddled her. Our eyes met, and I lost myself in her gaze. I was mesmerized. My hunger for her grew deeper. I had never experienced this before. "You do? And what is that?" I asked.

Claire gasped and arched her back as she inserted a finger into herself. "I've only begun to please myself since I've met you."

I lowered my body onto hers. "Is that so?"

She bit her lower lip and smiled. "Hmm, hmm." She moaned. "I've fantasized about this moment so many times. I can't believe this is real."

Her confession sent heated waves of passion through me. I couldn't hold back anymore. I wanted her and drew in deep breaths as I parted her legs. With ease, I slid myself into her and released a loud moan. "Tell me more about your fantasy." I moaned between short pants as I thrust my hips.

She gasped and arched her back. "God, you feel so damn good," she squealed. "I've wanted you for so long."

I pulled back and thrust again. Claire's body entwined with mine was pure bliss. It was better than I had ever imagined. It went deep. It connected us. What we experienced was more than just sex. "I've wanted you too. You feel amazing."

Claire matched my rhythm until I was riding her good and hard. She held onto my sides and dug her nails into my flesh, but I didn't winch. Instead, I pushed harder from the sting. Within minutes I peeked and reached an incredible, powerful orgasmic state.

Claire was seconds behind me and climaxed with a bang. She held nothing back and screamed at the top of her lungs, as she arched her back and thrust her pelvis up to meet me. "Yes! Yes. Oh, my fucking god Travis. You have no frigging idea how good this feels." Her body continued to jolt. "Hell yeah," she screamed.

I thrust hard once more. Exhausted and out of breath, I collapsed on top of her. Sweat dripped from my brow and chest. "Damn, girl. You came good." I said between heaves of breaths.

Claire panted, unable to speak. My head rested on her pounding chest. Finally, after a moment of catching her breath, she dropped her arms over my back and spoke. "That was frigging amazing." She gulped in some air. "I knew you were worth the wait," she laughed.

I lifted my head and gave her a smooch while she reaped air into her lungs. "I told you I wouldn't disappoint you," I snickered.

"Oh, you definitely didn't do that," Claire said as she wiped her moist brow with her forearm. She slid from underneath me and sat up. She glowed and wore a huge satisfied grin that warmed my heart. "Hey, do you want some ice cream?"

I pulled myself up and sat on the edge of the bed. I gloated and felt relaxed. I had no stress or anxiety. I could finally say I was happy. "Sure. What flavor do you have?"

"Only the best. Chocolate chip," she answered as she grabbed her bathrobe that hung on the bedroom door.

"My favorite," I said with a content smile. "I'm right behind you."

Claire paused at the doorway and looked over her shoulder. "Ooh, I like the thought of you behind me," she giggled. "You make a good roommate, by the way."

I threw her a loving smile as I pulled on my jeans. "You do too."

CHAPTER 9

CLAIRE

I know I didn't have much to compare with, but sex with Travis last night blew my mind. It's amazing what an incredible orgasm will do for the body and the soul. For the first time, I felt sexy. I wasn't ashamed of my body or shy. Just being in the same room with Travis had always sent my heart racing and the butterflies in my stomach to churn. When he came to me a free man, there was no longer a resistance between us. He undressed me with his dreamy eyes and seduced me with his touch. I had no desire to hold back. I had waited and dreamed about this moment for too long. I came unleashed, and I finally fed the burning hunger I had for this beautiful man.

After we pigged out on ice cream on the couch, we curled up next to each other in bed and spooned together underneath the sheets; I nuzzled my head under his chin and pulled his muscled arm tightly around my waist. Shielded by his magnificent body, I relaxed and closed my eyes.

Travis was the first man I had shared my bed with, and it turned out to be quite the adventure. I soon discovered he was a restless sleeper and talked in his sleep. We laid silently together for about fifteen minutes. I enjoyed the warmth of his breath on the back of my neck. It soothed me, and I drifted off to sleep. I'm not sure how long I had been sleeping, but when Travis mumbled slurred words in his sleep, I became conscious again. I laid still. My back still up against his chest and listened for any more strange sounds.

He broke free of our spoon position and flipped over, so he's back laid against mine. I rubbed my naked butt against his and giggled. A few minutes later, he turned and swung his arm across my face. With ease, I gently lifted it and wrapped it around my chest. I held his hand as I tried to fall asleep again.

I drifted off. I was in a half-conscious state, reminiscing about my recent love-making session with Travis. At first, I thought it was part of my dream when I heard Travis laugh and didn't stir. Then I heard. "Stop tickling me." I opened my eyes for the second time and glanced at the neon clock. I wasn't used to being awake at midnight. I'm usually asleep by eleven Travis laughed again and pulled his body away from mine and held his hands up to his chest and squealed with laughter.

I turned to face him; the room dimmed by the night light. I saw the outline of his face. "I'm not tickling you," I said with an edge.

He ignored me and continued to wave his arms.

I raised the tone of my voice a notch. "Travis. Did you hear me?" No answer. I studied his face, and even with little light, I saw his eyes were closed. "He's talking in his sleep," I whispered. I chuckled and thought it was cute. I leaned over and gently kissed him on the cheek. "Sweet dreams," I whispered and made some space between us.

Third time's a charm because the next thing I knew, I woke to the sun streaming through the gap of my curtains. I turned to face Travis and smiled. His eyes were closed and still asleep. I stared at him for a moment and admired his sexiness. Waking up to him every morning would undoubtedly brighten my mornings. The clock on the nightstand read seven o'clock. Tilly needed to go out soon. I wanted to take her out before she barked and woke Travis. I've never woken up with someone in my bed before. This was all new. I soon realized it would take some getting used to, especially if I am the first to wake up.

As I pulled back the sheets, I stayed focused on Travis and made sure I didn't disturb him. I was relieved I had not. I pulled my body upright and swung my legs over the edge of the bed and froze when the mattress squeaked. I held my breath and glanced at Travis. Pleased, I exhaled. The sound had not woken him. Once my feet were planted safely on the hardwood floor, I tiptoed across the room and grabbed my bathrobe off the back of the door. I looked once more over at the bed. Travis had not stirred. Proud with myself for not waking him, I wrapped myself in my bathrobe and quietly left the bedroom, closing the door softly behind me.

As soon as I went into the living room, Tilly was out of her bed barking. "Shh, Tilly!" I whispered harshly.

Amazingly, she stopped, gave her fur coat a good shake and. ran over to my feet, with her tail wagging profusely. "Okay. Okay, I'll take you outside," I said in a half-whisper. I smiled down at her and picked her up. Her dark brown eyes met mine as I gave her a peck on her cold, damp nose. "Come on, let's go," I said and grabbed her leash from the back of the door where it hung.

Ten minutes later, Tilly and I returned to the condo. I expected to have to be quiet again, but the sweet aroma of coffee invaded my nose as soon as I entered the apartment. "Travis." I hollered as I closed the door and hung up Tilly's leash.

Travis stuck his head out from the doorway of the kitchen, and Tilly ran toward him, barking. "Hey, good morning, beautiful." He smiled. "Would you like some coffee?" He asked.

I matched his smile. "Sure, I'd love some," Tilly continued to dance around his feet. I laughed at her cuteness before I put her on the couch.

I stood in the doorway and stared at Travis. I couldn't believe that such a handsome man had made love to me last night and shared my bed. And now here he stood in my kitchen, shirtless, wearing only faded jeans and making me coffee. How did I get to be so damn lucky?"

He looked over his shoulder in my direction with the coffeepot in his hand. "So, how did you sleep?" He asked before pouring two cups.

"Ha! Funny, you should ask." I walked over to him and placed my arms around his waist. I looked into his bright green eyes. "Do you know you talk in your sleep?" I said with a chuckle.

His eyes became wide. "Oh shit. I'm sorry. It happens when I'm in a strange bed." He locked his arms around my waist. "Did I keep you awake?"

I laughed and rolled my eyes. "Yeah, you could say that. I think I finally got to sleep around one."

Travis cocked back his head and briefly closed his eyes from guilt. "Shit, what did I say? It wasn't anything bad, was it?"

I shook my head and giggled. His sudden panic attack amused me. "No. You laughed about someone tickling you. It was quite comical. I've never known anyone that talks in their sleep before."

Travis creased his brow and then pulled away and added milk to his coffee. "Someone was tickling me? I don't remember a thing." He held up the milk jug, "Want milk?" He asked.

I shook my head. "No. I like it black."

Silence filled the kitchen as we savored our cups of coffee.

"So, it's only when you're in a strange bed that you talk in your sleep?" I asked before taking another sip of my drink.

Travis nodded. "Yep, seems to be. The hotels are terrible. You never want to sleep with me in one of those." He laughed again and took a sip of his coffee. "We should get separate rooms."

"Well, that will never happen. So how long will it take for my bed not to be a strange one?" I asked as I nuzzled up close to him, being careful not to spill my drink."

He rubbed his nose with mine, and I breathed in his scent as he spoke. "Let's hope not too long." He leaned down and gave me a gentle kiss on the lips. His lips were warm, and my knees went weak. My eyes closed for a few seconds, and when we separated, I found myself lost in his brilliant smile. "I don't want you to kick me out," he whispered.

I smiled back. "I enjoy having you around. I can't see that happening."

I was happy we had the weekend to adjust to our new living situation. We spent two days organizing Travis's things and made room for his clothes in my dresser and the closet.

There was limited space around the single sink in the bathroom. I stuffed all the unnecessary items in the cupboard below.

We took the tools he didn't use every day and stored them in the spare bedroom. After I helped him unload his larger tools, a chop saw drill press, air compressor, and a few ladders, the room suddenly appeared much smaller.

"I hope you have no more things somewhere else. If we keep this up, we will have to get a bigger place," I said with some uncertainty. My condo suddenly felt much smaller. There were now six pairs of shoes next to the front door instead of my four. Bags of tools that Travis didn't want to leave in the truck sat on the other side of the door. In the kitchen, my table that used to have only napkins and placemats now had two ice chests and a yellow water igloo sitting on it. "We need to find a place for these," I said while I scanned the kitchen and saw no floor space. "We can't leave them on the table. Where are we going to eat?"

"Do you have any cupboard space?" Travis asked. "There's no room on the floor," he said while scanning the kitchen. "Man, I sure do miss my garage," he confessed.

I let out a sarcastic laugh. "No! My cupboards are full." I went back into the living room and opened the sliding glass door. "We can store them on the balcony. There's only two chairs out here and a small table."

Travis agreed and left to retrieve his things from the kitchen table.

"I'm going to take a shower," I hollered from the other room and soon realized there were other things I should be concerned about with Travis.

I needed to be aware of Travis's living habits. I learned last night he snored and was a restless sleeper. After I closed the bathroom door, I sat on the toilet to take a pee. The frigid cold of the porcelain stung my ass, and I jumped up fast with my panties around my ankles. "Damn it," I yelled. I had not been in the habit of checking to see if the toilet seat was down. Now it looks like I needed to.

Travis heard my shrieks of frustrations. "Are you okay?" he asked from the other side of the door?"

"Yeah, I'm fine. I'll be out in a minute." I replied in a calmer tone as I noticed Travis's underwear and socks on the floor next to the sink. I shook my head and questioned why he hadn't put them in the hamper that was only two feet away. *Yup, living with a man was going to take some getting used to.* As I picked up his dirty laundry and threw it in the hamper, I shook my head again and then noticed the cap off the toothpaste. I cussed again, but this time in a whisper. "God damn it!" I searched for the lid and finally found it wedged in the sink's drain. "Fuck!" Before I could put it back on, I had to clean all the dried toothpaste crusted around the top. "Yuk! Disgusting!"

I returned to the living room, feeling somewhat irritated, and found Travis sitting on the couch with a second cup of coffee. I've never had to pick up after a man, and I wasn't about to start now. I took a seat next to him and placed my hand on his knee and gave him a sinister smile. "Hey, if you don't want me to kick you out, then don't leave the toilet seat up or the lid off the toothpaste and put your clothes in the hamper." I cocked my head and patted his thigh. "Got it?"

Travis lowered his head with guilt. "Oops, I'm sorry. Jill used to tell me the same thing."

I slapped his thigh again, but this time a little harder. His remark had stung, "And don't start comparing me to Jill." I felt my cheeks flush. "I'm nothing like her." And I don't need to be reminded of how your life with Jill was," I said in a sharper tone.

Travis furrowed his brow, "Hey, calm down. I'm sorry, okay."

I heaved my chest and folded my arms across my chest and didn't reply. I looked away and shook my head.

"What's going on?" he asked as he rubbed my thigh. "Don't start clamming up on me now. Let's talk about what's going on with you. You trust me, right? Let's not change that. Okay?"

I rolled my eyes and ran my hands through my hair and away from my face. "I'm sorry, okay. The stuff in the bathroom angered me, and then you brought up Jill, which pushed me over the edge." I stood up from the couch and paced the floor. Travis's eyes followed me. I turned to face him with my hands on my hips. "And do you know why I'm so upset by the mention of her name?"

Travis shrugged his shoulders. "Because she's my ex?"

I raised my voice a few notches and folded my arms across my chest. "No, Travis. It's because I have to work with her tomorrow. I'm dreading it."

"Oh shit! That's right. It's Monday tomorrow," he gasped.

"Yeah, it's Monday, all right," I said with sarcasm. "She doesn't know about us. How am I supposed to act like you and I don't exist? I thought things would be much easier once we were together. I hadn't thought about keeping us a secret from Jill. Things aren't any better Travis." My eyes turned misty, and I tried to sniff back the tears but failed and felt them run down my cheeks. "I can't lie, Travis. I don't know how." I circled the room with my hands back on my hips. "Yes, I've kept secrets, but I've never been dishonest" I suddenly had a horrifying thought and came to an abrupt stop. I turned to face Travis and gave him a hard stare. "What if she asks me if I know where you are?'

Travis stared back with a creased brow. "Why would she ask you? You told me you hardly speak to her."

"I don't know. She saw you helping me fix my car. Maybe she

thinks I would know." I held my hand up to my forehead and paced the room again. "She's going to find out eventually, and god knows what she will say to me when she does."

Travis left the couch and stopped me in my tracks. I lowered my head in distress as he placed a hand on each shoulder. "Hey, now. You're overthinking all of this and getting all wigged out. Do you want to take the day off tomorrow? I'll be starting a new job with Slater, and you could have the entire day to think all of this through."

I pushed Travis's hands away in disgust. "No, I don't want to take the day off. And then what, I take the next day and the next day off too?' I folded my arms. "At some point, we will have to tell her, or eventually, she will hear about us from someone else." I narrowed my lips and hissed my words. "I'd much rather she heard it from us."

Travis curled his lip. He looked nervous. "Let's wait awhile. It's only been a few days, and I'm sure she's still pissed off at the world right now. We should give it some time to allow the dust to settle." He gave me a questionable look. "Don't you think?"

I shook my head and raised my hands. "No, Travis, I don't think. I'm sick of hiding from the rest of the world. I want to show you off. I want to tell everyone that you are my man." I narrowed my eyes. "Don't you want to show me off, Travis?"

Travis shook his head slightly and attempted to approach me again. I took a step back. "Of course, I want to show you off," he stated. "Why did you back away from me? Are you that upset?"

"Yes, I am! I'm sick of this. Jill needs to be told. And if it doesn't happen soon, I swear I will tell her. You don't have to work with her, I do."

Travis's raised voice startled me. "Don't you think I know that Claire. It's why I've not told her about you. It's because you work with her. Don't you get it? I'm thinking about you, not frigging Jill, and what her reaction might be." He rolled his eyes and looked away. "I don't give a shit what Jill thinks. But I do worry about you going to work after she finds outs. She can be a real bitch, and if she can make your life miserable, trust me, she will. I know. She did it to me."

My mood softened. I had read Travis all wrong. I had it all backward and suddenly felt foolish. He was right. It was too soon to tell Jill. We needed some time to pass, so everything wasn't so new. I lowered my eyes and took a step towards him. "I'm sorry."

Travis took a step and gave me a subtle smile. He held out his hand, and I took it. "I'm just looking out for you."

I folded into his arms and gave him a loving smile. "I know that now," I said and gave him a peck on the lips. "I'm just eager to have a normal relationship with you without it being a secret. As it is right now, you can't come to my work at all until Jill knows about us. We're still living in secrecy, and I hate it."

"I hate it too. Listen, if you want us to tell her tomorrow, then we will. You're the one that has to see her every day. Not me, and I don't want you to be afraid of going to work."

I thought for a moment and placed my hands on his chest. "Nah, you're right. Let's wait for a while. If we tell her now, she'll probably have a shit-fit at work in front of everyone, and I couldn't handle that."

"Are you going to be okay working with her, though, until we do tell her?" Travis asked with concern.

"Yeah, I'll be fine. I don't see her much, except first thing in the morning. I'm good at keeping to myself. It's how I've lived most of my adult years."

Travis wrapped his arms around my shoulders and pulled me in tight. I snuggled up to his chest and breathed in his scent. "When you're ready to tell her, let me know, okay. We'll do it together. I don't expect you to fix my messes, okay?"

I nodded. "Okay."

The next morning though, I wasn't over it like I had thought. I woke up in a shitty mood and bitched that the coffee Travis had made was too strong. God, If I keep up with my picky ways, he's going to leave me, and I couldn't say I blame him. I drove to work, unable to shake the surge of guilt I'd experienced. I had snapped at Travis for stupid petty things, and it wasn't fair to him. I'd been so wound up about Jill. I'd done nothing but think about it all morning and had no idea what to expect when I walked through that door. For all I knew, she may already know about Travis and me.

After I parked my car, I sat for a few minutes and took some deep breaths of courage before I stepped out and locked the door.

When I entered the reception area, Jill was already at her station involved in an in-depth conversation with the new girl, Sadie. She nodded. "Hi, Claire." And went back to talking to Sadie.

I returned the nod and said a simple hello, but it was apparent she hadn't heard me and continued to walk to the back of the building to the x-ray room. *Huh? I guess I had nothing to worry about. Well, not yet anyway.*

CHAPTER 10

TRAVIS

Over the next month, Claire and I adjusted to our new living arrangements. I had to be honest; We struggled. Living with someone new hadn't been easy, and I had to keep checking with Claire to see how she was doing with the sudden changes in her life.

"So, are you doing okay?" I asked her the other night over dinner.

We were sitting on the couch, eating Chinese food, and she turned to me and smiled. "I'm doing good. Are you okay?"

I matched her smile and nodded. "Yeah, I am. I'm happy."

She nudged my upper arm with hers. "Me too."

"And you're okay with us living together, anything you want to talk about or tell me something that pisses you off?" I joked.

Claire chuckled with a mouth full of rice and swallowed before she spoke. "I'm adjusting but in a good way. You're getting good at putting the cap back on the toothpaste and not leaving the toilet seat up. I think I've only had to put it down once as for the laundry on the floor. We still need to work on that," she said with a sarcastic grin. She patted my knee. "I love you being here. I think it's working out fine."

I let out a contented sigh. "This is what I like about us."

"What's that?"

"We talk to each other. We work things out. You tell me what bothers you, and I don't make fun of your little pet peeves."

Her eyes grew wide. "What pet peeves? I don't have any pet peeves."

A snort escaped my nose when I laughed. "Yes, you do. You have to make the bed every day. No matter what time it is. Even if it's nine o'clock at night."

She gave me a friendly slap on my shoulder. "Well, I don't like getting into an unmade bed. It feels weird. And you're making fun of me."

I laughed louder. "But we're going to get in anyway. I don't get it." I raised my hands. "But, hey, it's your thing."

Claire nodded in triumph. "Yes, it is my thing, so quit making fun of me."

I gave her a loving smile. "I'm not making fun of you. I'm just saying."

Claire shook her head. "Okay, enough. Eat your food—no more talk about my pet peeves.

I leaned in and gave her a peck on the cheek. "See what I mean. We talk about ourselves. I frigging love it."

Me on the other hand. It's my ego that has taken a toll. This is her home, not mine, and I've continued to have a sense of not belonging no matter how much Claire has tried to make me feel welcomed. I've always taken care of my women by making sure the bills had been paid, doing all the yard work - here, there is no yard to take care of and no home improvement projects for me to tackle, which has always been a boost for my ego. Every week I've given her money towards the bills. It bothers me that she handles the money. She's been an independent woman ever since she left home. I can't see that changing anytime soon. I won't pressure Claire with these things. She is gradually letting me into her world at her pace. And that's okay. Eventually, we will meet in the middle.

Even though we've gone through a lot of changes, there's one thing we have in stock, and that is the sparkle in our eyes when we see each other. I can't wait to get home to see her after working all day on the mansion job with Slater. The minute I see her, I have to pick her up and spin her around before giving her a heart-warming smooch and tell her how much I've missed her. Her laughter warms my heart, and the evenings we spend snuggled on the couch under a blanket and sometimes with Tilly makes all the struggles we've dealt with worth-while.

We've still not told Jill about us. I've asked Claire several times how things are at work, and Jill has become best buddies with the new girl, Sadie, and she has moved into the condo with her. Claire has kept to herself like she always had and didn't see the need to rock the boat and tell her about us. *"Eventually, we will tell her. I'm kind of waiting until she comes in and announces that she is seeing someone. The more time that goes by, the better right. Don't you think?"* Claire asked me. I wanted to tell Jill the truth about Claire and me and be the man I want to be. It's been rough not being able to visit her at work whenever I wanted to. I can't believe how much I miss her when we are apart. But she has to work there, not me, so whatever she wants to do I'll go along with.

The sudden changes in our lives had been a challenge, and we hadn't taken many timeouts for us. I'd been working long hours for Slater at Eve's job—who is Slater's ex. And on weekends we've hung out at home and made some improvements. I built some more shelves in the closet—which was good for my ego and some extra shelves in the bedroom. It felt good to do something for Claire, finally. But I wanted to do more.

"I want to take you somewhere today," I said to her on this Saturday morning as we sat on the couch in each other's arms with our coffee watching the morning news. "Just you and me. It's time we had some fun together." I beamed her a smile. "What do you say?"

Claire returned the smile. "Sounds good to me. I need to spend a day outdoors."

"Great. Do you have any favorite places? If so, I'll take you to one of those."

A devious smile appeared on her face. "Well, there is one place that I've been missing. It's a place where I can be me without judgment."

"Really? Well I'm Intrigued. Where is this amazing place?" I asked.

She tossed back her head and giggled childishly. "Promise you won't laugh."

"Of course not. Now enough with the suspense and tell me." I said as I sneaked a quick tickle to her hip.

She jolted and laughed. "I want to go to Day's Beach," she said, almost in a whisper.

"The nude beach?" I said, stunned by her answer.

Her jaw dropped. "You know about Day's Beach?"

I laughed. "I sure do. I've not been there since I began dating Jill. I used to love that place." I looked at her with a creased brow. "You go there by yourself?"

"I did everything by myself. You know that. I stumbled on the nude beach by accident and noticed all the different varieties of people." She nudged my arm. "It's not just for people with perfect bodies, you know. Anyway, I thought, well, I'm already here, so why not?" She cracked a laugh and snorted, "It was the best thing I'd ever done on the spur of the moment. It's a place where I'm accepted as me and not judged by anyone. I wear only my big floppy sun hat and shades and lie under the sun naked. I swim in the ocean, I read books, I pack a lunch, and I'm accepted by all the people around me, unlike how I feel in the city."

I slapped my knees and stood up. "Well, then let's go. I have parts of my body that have not seen the sun in years."

Claire laughed before leaving the couch. "Sweet, I can't believe we both like nude beaches."

It took us about an hour to pack everything and take Tilly out to go potty before we got on the road. The beach was about thirty minutes away, and we made good timing and arrived there before ten o'clock.

It wasn't crowded, and we found the perfect spot from the water.

I looked up at the glorious blue sky and breathed in the fresh air. "Man, it feels good to be here. I'd forgotten how rejuvenating it feels," I told Claire as we laid down the towels.

"Yeah, I've missed it too."

"The last time I came here, I was alone. I won't do that again."

"Why? I've never had a problem coming here on my own."

"Yeah, but you're a woman. I was a single guy, and that doesn't go over too well at nude beaches, let me tell you. People looked at me like I was some pervert looking for a cheap thrill. No one smiled at me or said hello. Talk about feeling uncomfortable in my own skin."

"But I thought you said you loved this place?"

"Yeah but only when I was with someone. Before I started dating Jill, I came here with other women and I was accepted. I tried coming once on my own and it didn't go over too well. Jill had made it clear she had no interest in going. Single guys are not welcomed here." Travis scanned the beach, "Look around. It's all couples, and I see a few single girls. Maybe there's some single men way off in the distance where they can't be seen." He chuckled.

Claire scoped their surroundings. "You know, you're right. I've never noticed that before."

I watched with admiration as Claire stripped down. She didn't hesitate at all. She was in her element. She showed a side of her that I rarely see—Confident and proud. As she stood naked on the towel, she held her head high and out to the wind as she breathed in the fresh air with her arms out like a bird. Her breasts faced the sun and soaked up the rays that beamed down on her. My eyes traveled down to her perfectly shaped butt that called out to my hands. My chest heaved. She was stunning.

"God, smell that air," she said as she filled her lungs and did a 360.

I undressed without taking my eyes off her. I couldn't. I'd never seen Claire stripped of all her insecurities and acted so free. It was a beautiful site that enhanced her beauty inside and out and sent my heart racing.

She was by far the most gorgeous woman on the beach. She had told me the truth. No one judged her. But what amazed me more was that Claire hadn't judged or compared herself to others. The transformation had been mesmerizing. Just when I had thought I knew her, I witnessed an incredible side of her that blew me away. Man, it just keeps getting better.

I stripped down and took her in my arms. "God, you are beautiful, kiss me."

She wrapped her arms around my neck and kissed me hard. "Thank you for allowing me to be me," she said in a whisper after ending the kiss.

I gave her a loving smile. "Sweetheart, I wouldn't want you to be anything else. It's why I'm so love-struck with you." I kissed her again. "Now, do you want to soak up some rays first or go for a swim?" I asked.

"I want to lie naked with you under the sun," she replied with a sultry smile. She took my hand and pulled me down next to her on the towel. Our thighs touched as we made ourselves comfortable and laid on our stomachs. Her skin was already warm from the rays of the sun, and she looked stunning. Sweat beaded on her back and trickled down the center of her spine. "Do you want me to rub some suntan oil on you?" I asked while rubbing her back.

She folded her arms in front of her and rested her chin on her hands. "I want to scan the beach and take it all in first."

I joined her and, like her, rested my chin on my hands. "Not too many people here yet. It's a good thing we got here early." I said as I looked at our surroundings.

Claire giggled.

"What's funny?" I asked as I tilted my head to face her.

"I wonder if we've ever been here on the same day before we knew each other?"

"Oh, wow! There's a possibility we may have. But I'm sure I would have remembered you."

Claire threw me a smile and nudged my side with her hip. "I know I would have remembered you too." She said and returned to check out others on the beach. "Oh, I see the exhibitionists are here."

I looked over to where she was looking. "The who?"

"Over there, under the big blue umbrella with yellow smileys on it." She said and tried to point discreetly with her head. "Every time I have come here on a Saturday, they've been here."

"Do you know them?"

"I know them from their live sex shows here on the beach." Claire laughed, "so does everyone else here on the beach, too, I imagine."

"You're kidding. Do they have sex in front of everyone? I've got to see this." I shifted my body, so I had a better view.

Claire dropped her jaw at my remark and gave my hip another nudge, but a little harder. "Travis!"

I laughed. "What? You've seen them. I haven't." I inched my torso closer to hers. "Were you turned on when you watched them?" I whispered, followed by a snarky grin.

She turned her body to face mine and gave me a good hard slap on my ass. "Travis! Will you stop?" And then her jaw dropped, and her eyes bulged, stretching her eyes sockets to the max as she looked past my shoulder. "Oh shit! Are you kidding me?"

My back faced where she focused her stare, and I struggled to pull myself up to see what she was looking at. "What is it?"

She didn't answer. "Where's my hat and shades?" She said in a panicked state. She turned and spotted them on the towel. Within seconds she had them on and grabbed my arm. "Don't look over there. Just lay on your stomach and hide your face in your arms," she said with a sense of urgency as she laid on her back and covered her face with her hat.

"Who's over there?" I whispered after I had laid back down.

"It's friggin' Slater and Sabela. They're walking right toward us." She whispered as she adjusted her sunglasses and held on to her hat.

My Jaw dropped. "You're fucking kidding! Oh shit. What if they see us?"

Claire turned her head slightly and peaked from behind her shades. "They're going up behind us, closer to the rocks. God, I hope they don't recognize us. How embarrassing will that be?" She patted my thigh. "Just lay still. I can't see them now. But you can. Where are they going?"

I couldn't help but feel like a peeping Tom as I peered above my arms without raising my head. "They're standing and looking around. It looks like they are looking for a place to sit. Oh god, please don't come next to us," I said with a dominant nervous laugh.

Finding the humor in our situation, Claire chuckled. "Can you believe this? I have never seen anyone I know here. What are they doing now, and why are they here?"

"That's odd," I said as I watched Sabela point at something.

"What is?" Claire asked in a whisper after hearing my serious tone.

"Sabela just pointed to the couple with the umbrella. "Do you think they know them?"

"I doubt it. Maybe she's just admiring it."

I felt my cheeks blush. "Oh, shit!"

"What?" Claire said in a desperate whisper.

"They're getting undressed. I don't want to see Slater naked. I'll never look at him the same way again." I ducked my head into my arms. "I can't watch."

Claire snickered at my embarrassment. "What the hell are we going to do? I feel so uncomfortable. I can't lie here and hide all day."

I peeked above my arms again and couldn't help but notice what a knockout Sabela was naked. They stood facing each other, wrapped in an embrace. I was just thankful that Sabela hid most of Slater's nakedness. I still felt like a peeping tom but continued to stare when they kissed, but as soon as they broke away, I quickly ducked my head down to avoid seeing Slater's junk. "Oh shit, they're coming this way," I said in a loud whisper.

"What? Keep your head low," Claire said as she adjusted her hat some more.

With my head still buried in my arms, I could hear Sabela's giggles getting closer. *Please don't come here. Please.* I froze as I tried to detect which way they were heading and soon sensed them walking right by us toward the ocean. "I think they're going for a swim," I whispered without moving my head.

"Shh. Don't let them see us."

After a few minutes had passed, I raised my head and looked over in the water's direction. "I see them out there. What do you want to do?"

Claire sat up and removed her shades. "I think we should go. What do you think?"

"Yeah, I'm with you. It's just too weird." I turned over and quickly grabbed my shorts. "Come on, I'll take you out for lunch, and then we can go home and have our own fun nude session."

Claire grinned. "Sounds good. Let's get out here before they see us."

CHAPTER 11

CLAIRE

Travis and I had our stuff packed within five minutes and were back in my car by ten, and that's when we let loose. We laughed so hard that we had tears streaming down our faces.

"Oh my god, Travis, I can't think of any other time in my life where I wanted to bury my head in the sand, and I mean literally." I squealed between high-pitched laughs.

Travis wiped his face dry with his hand. "It's going to be weird going back to work Monday and seeing Slater. I don't know if I can keep a straight face."

"Well, if you don't want him to know, you'd better." I cracked another loud laugh and smacked his thigh and laughed again when my glasses fell off my face.

"Oh, I'll never tell him about this. I can guarantee you that. Now let's find a place to eat. I'm starving."

"Sounds good."

After a good hearty steak and shrimp lunch, we decided we would have our nudist session at home and watch a movie. "Well, if we can't be naked at the beach, we sure as hell can be naked at home. Right?" I said as I turned on to my street.

Travis rubbed my thigh. "You've got that right, babe."

My condo was halfway down the street, and as I slowed down to turn into the covered carport, I looked to my left and saw an older couple sitting in a car outside my building. I strained my eyes to see if I recognized them. The man in the driver's seat turned and looked at me. I slammed on the brakes and gasped, "Oh my god! That's my dad."

Travis peered over my shoulder. "What?"

I wound down my window at the same time my dad rolled down his. I looked beyond my dad and saw my mom. Tears ran down her cheeks.

"What are you doing here?" I asked, my voice cold and flat.

From what I could tell, he had lost a lot of weight. I never remembered his cheekbones being so prominent. His eyes had lost their sparkle, and his hair was now almost grey. "We need to talk." He said in a solemn tone.

My heart skipped a beat as he spoke. "Dad, I think we said enough already, don't you think?"

My dad slammed his hands on the steering wheel. Mom reached over and squeezed his shoulder. "Jeffery, please!" She sniffed between tears.

My dad shook his shoulder and shrugged her away. He gave me a hard, icy stare. "God damn it, Claire! I've had enough of this nonsense. They sentenced your brother to another twenty years. Your mother and I do not want to lose our daughter too."

Tears flowed down my dad's cheeks. I wasn't used to seeing him cry. My mom sobbed in the background, echoed loudly in my ears.

"Please, Claire! Let us talk to you. We want to apologize. Please give us a few minutes of your time. We love you," he said in a desperate plea.

I felt Travis' hand on my thigh. "Claire, talk to them," he whispered.

I turned to face him. Tears gushed down my cheeks. "I don't know if I can."

Travis leaned over and gently wiped away my tears and kissed me tenderly on the lips. "Yes, you can. They are your parents. Everyone needs a mom and dad in their lives. Trust me when I say that. I miss mine every day."

"Where are your parents?" I asked between tears.

"I'll tell you another time. You need to fix things with your parents and find out what happened to your brother." He raised his voice a notch as he squeezed my thigh. "I'm sorry, but I can't stand to see this. You are lucky to have your parents still around. I don't want you to regret anything when they are gone." He gave my thigh a hard squeeze. "Please invite them up, and let's try to salvage your relationship with them."

I had never tried to fix my relationship with my parents. I had accepted a life without them. They made their decision to support Davin, and I couldn't be a part of that. So what changed? Why are they here now? I needed to know, and I wanted to hear their side of things. Maybe Travis was right? Am I ready to have them be a part of my life again? I honestly didn't know if I could.

I turned to face my parents. "Let me go park, and I'll come out and get you," I said, using a flat tone.

My dad released a sigh and gave my mother an encouraging smile. "Thank you, Claire. We'll wait here."

I nodded and drove away. I clutched the steering wheel hard until my knuckles turned white. "I'm not sure if this is a good idea, Travis," I uttered.

Travis reached over and squeezed my hand. "Yes, it is. Trust me."

I shook my head with uncertainty and parked the car in silence.

I checked my face in the rearview mirror and adjusted my glasses. Travis stepped out and stood at my opened door.

He held out his hand. "Leave the stuff in the car. We'll come back and get it later. Your parents are waiting."

I took his hand and stepped out, "Okay."

He didn't let go of my hand; instead, he took the other one and held them together up to his chin. "You can do this, Claire. You'll be fine."

I shook my head again. I wasn't so sure. "What do I say to them?" I said as we held hands through the parking structure. "I've not spoken to them in over two years."

"You will know once the conversation begins. I know they've hurt you, and they know that too. They are trying to make amends with you. Let them have their say and see how you feel afterward. Okay?"

I nodded. "Okay."

My parents stood at the bottom of the steps. I stopped for a second and took a deep breath before I approached them. My mom had also aged. She allowed her hair to grow out to its natural color and now gray. Like my father, her eyes looked lifeless and red from her tears. She lost weight too. I remembered the navy blue dress she wore. But now it looked a few sizes too big.

Before I could react, my mom embraced me. She wrapped her arms tight around my waist. She buried her head into my chest and cried hysterically. "Oh, Claire, I've missed you so much. Your father and I are sorry." She sniffed back her tears. "Please forgive us," she begged.

I rejected her embrace. I froze. My arms limp at my sides while my mom continued to weep. My dad saw my uneasiness and tugged at my mom's arm. "Get a hold of yourself, Abigail."

My mom tried to shake him off, but his hold was too strong and pulled her away from me. "Give her some space. Let's go inside where we can talk," he ordered.

My dad locked eyes with me for just a second, but it was more than enough to weaken me as I read the sadness in his stare. "I'm sorry, Claire. Your mom can't take much more."

Numbness overwhelmed my body. Unable to move, I stood in silence.

Travis rubbed my shoulders and took the lead. "Come on, let's go inside and I'll make us a pot of coffee."

I nodded and followed him up the front steps.

My mom pulled a tissue from her purse and dabbed her eyes. She locked arms with my dad and followed Travis through the entranceway. Her eyes gave Travis a forced, subtle smile. "Thank you."

I entered the building last. I remained silent and stayed a few steps behind everyone. My mind was in a tailspin, unsure how to react to this unexpected visit from my parents. For the past two years, I lived my life on my terms without answering to anyone. I adjusted to not having parents and distanced myself as the sister of a rapist. I had not spoken often of his name. He became a distant memory and I had finally lived my life from beneath his shadow.

What would happen if I reconnected with my parents and allowed them to be a part of my life? Would things return to how they used to be? I won't go back to living that way. I refused. I've worked so hard to get to where I am. I've never been this happy, and I'll be damned if I should sacrifice my happiness for my parents.

As we walked down the corridor in silence, I clenched my fist to help subside the anger I felt towards them. I was unsure if I could ever forgive them for not loving me like they loved Davin. They were never there for me, and now they expect me to put my feelings aside and be there for them. I'm sorry for their pain. But I've been hurting since I was a little girl and no one came to my rescue.

Travis had the key to the condo, and we heard Tilly barking on the other side.

"You have a dog?" My dad asked.

"Yes. She's friendly," I mumbled.

Travis eased the door open and grabbed Tilly before she

escaped and tucked her under his arm. He gave her a peck on the nose. "Hey girl." I motioned my parents inside. When I walked by, he brushed my hand with his and whispered. "It'll be okay."

I rolled my eyes. "Easy for you to say," I whispered back.

As soon as Travis closed the door, my heart thumped hard beneath my chest. I wasn't sure if I was ready for this. I curled my fingers and felt the sweat on my palms. I looked over at Travis and pleaded with my eyes for him to say something and break the unbearable silence in the room. Travis understood and took leadership."

He looked over at my parents and motioned with his arm to the couch. "Have a seat."

My dad nodded, "Thank you." His voice was humble. He sat beside my mom and held her hand.

Travis looked my way and handed me, Tilly. "Do you want to put her in the bedroom for a while?" He asked.

I nodded and left the room, relieved. I had an excuse to leave for a minute. When I returned, Travis stood in the middle of the room, and my parents sat on the couch.

He rubbed his hands together. "Okay, I'll go make a pot of coffee."

My heart raced. My nerves were on edge at the mere thought of being along with my parents. I dashed to Travis's side. "Can I help you?" I pleaded.

"Er, sure." He glanced over at my parents. "We'll be right back."

In the kitchen, I heaved my chest and exhaled hard. I leaned against the sink and folded my arms. "Why are they here?" I whispered in a harsh voice.

Travis stood next to me at the sink as he filled the coffee pot with water. "Because they are your parents. They are here to make amends. Give them a chance," he stated.

I spat out my words in a harsh whisper. "Well, they have a funny way of showing it. You have no idea what my childhood was like."

He gave me a bitter stare. "At least you know your parents. Many kids don't have that luxury. You're lucky in so many ways and don't even realize it."

"What's that supposed to mean?" I replied, matching his tone.

Travis rolled his eyes as he poured the water into the coffee machine and added coffee to the filter. After he gave me a cold stare and faced me, he gripped me hard on the shoulders and gave me a sharp shake. "You need to make things right with your parents, Claire."

I pushed him away with the palms of my hand. I was disgusted that he was backing my parents and not me. My cheeks flushed. It enraged me. How dare he? "I don't have to do anything, Travis!" I said louder than I intended.

Then I heard my father call from the other room. "Maybe we should leave. We could talk another time?"

Travis ignored my protest and rushed to the living room. "No. No. Everything is fine. We're just waiting for the coffee. You sit right there," he said and returned to the kitchen just as quickly as he had left.

He gave me another bitter stare. "You're doing this, and you will thank me later. Trust me." He scanned the kitchen, not waiting for a protest. "Do you have a tray anywhere?"

I gritted my teeth. "Why should I trust you? Why are you making me do this?" I folded my arms and shook my head. "You have no idea what they put me through," I snarled.

Travis forgot about looking for the tray and spun around. His eyes narrowed, and his nostrils flared. "No, I don't, Claire, but I'll be damned if I'm going to sit back and watch you destroy this chance of reconciling with them." He leaned in closer until his nose touched mine. "They have made the first move by coming here. The least you can do is listen to what they have to say." He scanned the kitchen again. "Now, do you have a tray or not?" he snapped.

"Fine," I moaned. But I didn't believe I would thank him later. I was sure I'd be telling him, *I told you so.* "The tray is between the fridge and the cabinet." I didn't like his plan and spoke with an edge to my voice. "I'll get the cream and sugar," I said as I nudged him out of my way with my hip.

I followed Travis closely into the living room and stood behind him as he placed the tray on the coffee table. "Here you go," he said, followed by a forced smile. He then turned to face me and spoke to me in a stern voice. "Claire, do you want to do the honors?"

I narrowed my eyes and glared at him. "If you insist." I looked at my mom, who dabbed her eyes with a tissue. "Black right, mom?" I asked as I picked up a coffee cup. It rattled in my hand from my unsettled nerves, and I quickly placed it on the coffee table before I poured the coffee.

She smiled. "You remembered."

"I did." Unsure what to say next. I quickly grabbed the other cups and filled them with coffee while everyone watched on in silence. I took a sip.

My father spoke first. "I'm sorry, Claire, that we couldn't call first, but you've changed your number. I planned on leaving you a note, but the guy that answered the door in your old apartment said you moved to a different unit, and he wasn't sure which one."

He turned and gave my mom a reassuring glance. "We were willing to wait outside all day until we saw you."

I stood my ground and didn't let my mom's continuous flow of tears break me. "So, what's this about?" I asked in a stiff tone.

Travis butted in. "Let's sit down Claire and talk to each other and not at one another." he urged and pulled the two ottomans out from beneath the coffee table.

I didn't answer and slid my butt onto the seat. Travis reached across and squeezed my thigh. I was still upset that I was in the room against my will, and I blamed Travis. I inched away from his annoying squeeze and placed my hands in my lap. My tone of voice remained cold. "Well?" I asked.

My father gave my mom another glance. "Davin was sentenced to an additional twenty years for three more rape charges that they have convicted him of in Texas."

I gasped. "What? Are you serious?" It was then that I realized, not by choice but by the state of Texas—I no longer had a brother. By the time he gets out, I will be in my late forties. We will be strangers. His threatening letters popped into my head. He had known all along he would not be getting out in seven years. They were all empty threats. He was trying to make me feel guilty so that I would visit him. I was numb and had to force myself to speak. "I knew he was a monster, and this just proved it even more." I shook my head in disgust. "So he raped three more women. Where?"

"We didn't go to the trial, Claire. From what I understand, all of them happened at the University, and they came forward after they had sentenced him for the first three. They were afraid to come forward until after the trial and knew he would be locked up."

"You didn't go to the trial? Why? You've always been there for him." I asked in a sarcastic tone.

My dad shook his head. "Not anymore. I'm ashamed to call him my son. Your mother and I are drained physically and mentally. We can't do it anymore, Claire. It's going to kill us."

I almost caved and wept for them. They looked fragile, sitting across from me on my couch. It was harder than I thought. I stood my ground and talked with no emotions. "So what's this got to do with me? You already know what I think about him. I was done with him the day I walked out of that courtroom." I paused. "And you too, for that matter."

"Claire, that's enough," Travis said, trying to use a calmer tone than mine.

I turned to face Travis and snarled at him. "Mind your own business, Travis. It has nothing to do with you." I leaned in until my breath bounced off his face when I spoke. "You have no idea what it was like growing up in a household where I was told all the time that I wasn't good enough or I wasn't pretty enough. Where my older brother could do no wrong and was born with a damn silver spoon in his mouth."

This time it was my mother that spoke. She let go of my father's hand and shook her head hard and gave me a hard stare. "Claire, your father and I made mistakes. I won't deny that. Davin was our firstborn, and like most new parents, we smothered him, and as it turns out, it ruined him too."

I interrupted my mother. Her words angered me. "Mom, you are not responsible for Davin's action. Don't you ever think that way."

My mother turned her head away in shame.

"Do you hear me?" I repeated. No matter how upset I was with my parents, I didn't want them to live the rest of their lives, thinking they were to blame for Davin's conviction.

My mom turned and looked at me. Her stare had softened, and she gave me a simple nod and then spoke in a softer tone. "Claire, we want you back in our lives. We can't bear to lose another child." My mom retook my dad's hand and gave him a loving smile. "We cut all ties with Davin. We will not be visiting him in prison or writing to him. I will ignore any letters I receive from him. As your father said, we can't do it anymore." She paused and took in a deep breath. "Your father has already had one minor heart attack from all of this. I'm afraid the stress of it all will kill him if we continue to let Davin be a part of our lives."

I gasped. "Dad had a heart attack?" Guilt swam through me as tears trickled down my cheeks. "Oh, my god. I had no idea."

My mom gave me a subtle smile. "How could you? You've not been in our lives, Claire."

"When did this happen?" I asked, still feeling chilled and numb from the shocking news.

"About two months ago, when we found out about Davin's

sentencing. It just broke him. I haven't written because I've been too busy taking care of your father, and not only that, it's something we wanted to tell you in person, which is another reason we are here."

As I listened to my mom talk of my father's near-death experience, Travis took my hand. This time I didn't pull away. Instead, I squeezed it hard. "It's okay to cry, Claire. You've kept so much in for so long." Travis said.

My mom grasped her hands together. Tears wallowed in her eyes. "We want you in our lives again, Claire. Don't deny us that, please."

I turned my head to hide my tears; I was breaking. It was too much.

Travis tightened his grip on my hand. "Your parents are begging you. Don't deny them their daughter and don't deny yourself your parents."

I looked at Travis and bit my lip and then over at my parents. My mother gave me a caring smile. I didn't know what to say. I was hesitant to make peace. Afraid I may get hurt again. Travis's words kept rolling around in my head. *Don't deny them their daughter.* That's what I was doing. But I hadn't looked at it that way. I had only thought about my feelings.

Travis was right, and now I wondered what to say next. Travis saw I struggled with expressing my emotions and gave my arm a little nudge. "Why don't you go give your mom and dad a hug," he whispered, followed by a sweet smile. "I think they could use one, and I think you could too."

Travis didn't wait for an answer from me or give me a chance to protest. Instead, he took my hand and two steps towards my parents. "Come on; I'll help you up."

My parents stood up from the couch and met me half-way. By the time we reached the middle of the room, our arms had opened, and tears gushed from all of us.

My mother embraced me first. "Oh, Claire, I'm so sorry. I love you so much."

I had missed her motherly love and security of her arms wrapped around me. I soon realized, no matter how old we are, we all still need our parents. I held on to my mom, tight and drenched her shoulder with my tears. "I'm so sorry, mom. I've always been so jealous of Davin, and when you continued to support him after…"

My mom interrupted me. "Shh, Claire. You don't need to explain." She opened up one of her arms to allow my dad into our embrace. It was a rare moment to see my dad cry hysterically. When I draped my arm over his shoulders, it stunned me to feel how skinny he felt. He used to have some meat on his shoulders, now they felt like skin and bones.

I was so overwhelmed and lost at the moment that I forgot about Travis until he spoke.

"I'm so happy I was here to witness this," Travis said. "All of you have been through so much. You need to support each other through these hard times and not fight."

I broke away from my parents and turned to face him. "Thank you," I said as I took his hand.

He smiled. "Why are you thanking me?"

"Because you made this happen. You know me better than I know myself." I took his other hand and entered his space where he then embraced me and kissed the top of my head. "If you weren't here, I probably wouldn't have invited my parents up. I would have been my usual stubborn self who refuses to admit when they are wrong."

Travis gave me another smile and glanced at my parents, who had returned to the couch hand in hand. "You just needed a little shove. The rest you did on your own."

I nodded. "Well, thank you for that," I said before glancing over at my mom and dad.

I lowered my head in shame. "I'm sorry for the way I've treated you both. Can we start over by allowing Travis and me to take you out to dinner?" I looked up and gave Travis a loving smile. "I want to show off my new boyfriend to you."

"We would love that," my dad said before wiping away one last trailing tear.

CHAPTER 12

TRAVIS

Claire didn't have to thank me. I did what anyone would have done if they'd witnessed what I had seen. It was sad to watch, and I couldn't let it go on anymore. They say that your eyes are the windows to your soul. The love seeped out of Claire's when she saw her parents sitting in their car outside the condo. But when she noticed I had been watching her, she soon hardened up. But it was too late; I had already seen the truth in her eyes. Claire just needed to open up to her genuine feelings, and it took some persuasion, but eventually, she did.

Claire and I sat in the back of her parent's car, and her father drove. The ride to the steak house felt awkward. The conversation came in pieces as Claire, and her parents learned to communicate again. I wanted them to reconnect and remember what they used to have. I initiated many of the conversations after moments of uncomfortable silence. "Do you live far from here?" I asked.

Jeffery shifted in his seat and bought his hand up to his mouth to cover a nervous cough. "No, actually, we don't. We live about thirty minutes away, near Camp Pendleton."

I turned to Claire, "You never told me they lived so close."

"Well, considering we weren't talking, I didn't think it was necessary," she replied with a hint of sarcasm.

I met her tone. "Well, now that you made amends, you'll be able to see them more often."

She took my hand and corrected me. "We can see them more often. I want to include you in everything I do. My parents have never seen me with someone as fabulous as you." She beamed me a big smile. "I want to show you off and let them see how happy you make me."

I leaned over and gave her a deep smooch, flattered by her confession. "You make me very happy too."

We arrived at the restaurant twenty minutes later. The sun had set, but the air was filled with warmth and we asked for a table outside on the deck.

After ordering our drinks, Claire began the conversation. "So, what do you know about Davin's latest charges?"

I was surprised to see her mom, Abigale, answer. Making peace with Claire had given her the strength she lacked. Her voice no longer cracked, and she sat with her shoulders straight instead of crouched over. "We only know what we told you." She looked at Jeffery. "I've come to terms that he is a sick man, a serial rapist. I can't imagine the damage he has done to those poor women."

I released a satisfactory smile as Claire reached across the table and took her mother's hand. "I'm so sorry I turned against you and wasn't there to give you my support. You and dad went through all of this on your own. No wonder dad had a heart attack."

"Claire. Honey, you did what you had to do for your sanity and well-being." Abigale released a slight chuckle. "It's funny, but strangely I'm jealous that you had the strength to walk away. Looking back, I wish your father and I did."

"It wasn't easy, mom. I've missed you, but as long as Davin was in your life, I couldn't be. It was that simple. I'll never forgive him for what he did."

"We won't either, Claire," Abigale said defiantly. "Not now. Not ever."

Claire looked skeptical. "Mom, he's your firstborn."

"It makes no difference now. He's a monster and no longer a son of ours."

When Abigale didn't shed a single tear and kept her jawline tight while describing her son as a monster, I sensed she was speaking from the heart. She no longer had any emotional ties to her son Davin. Her voice was cold and harsh. I sensed hatred in her tone as she spat out her words, and then Jeffery spoke for the first time since we had sat down. He looked at both of us from across the table.

"We may have ruined Davin by giving him everything he wanted and catered to his every need, but I see now I was trying to relive my youth through him. Before he had turned five, I had his future carved out duplicating my high school and then sending him off to Rice University." He focused his stare on Claire. "You're the smart one in the family, Claire. You saw what we were doing before I did, and being the smart woman that you are, you were able to break the mold by being able to make your own decisions and not allow anyone to judge you" He reached over and grabbed her other hand. It was a beautiful sight to see, Claire holding a hand of each parent. "I'm damn proud of you, Claire, and I'm sorry for not saying that sooner," her Father said.

It touched my heart when I saw Claire's eyes mist up. "Thanks, dad, that means a lot." She shook her head and composed herself. She fought the tears that pooled her eyes. "Okay, before we get emotional again, let's' order," she said, her voice still shaken.

After we placed our order, Claire's parents turned to me. "So, Travis, what do you do?"

I put my arm around Claire's shoulder, and I gave her a loving smile. "I'm in construction."

Jefferey nodded. "Well, when I want to do some remodeling, I'll look you up."

I returned the nod. "Sounds good. I'll give you a good deal."

And then Abigale asked the question I had been waiting for. "So, where did you two meet, and have you been dating long?"

"Your daughter was a damsel in distress with a broken-down vehicle, and I saved her." I chuckled. I looked at Claire before I spoke again. "As far as how long we've been together, in the beginning, it was complicated. I moved in with Claire a few months ago."

Abigale leaned back and smiled. It was good to see her smile. "Well, I think you are a good looking couple. I like you, Travis." She said with a nod.

"Thank you, Abigale. That means a lot." I turned and gave Claire a peck on the cheek.

While we waited for our food, we talked more about Davin. The subject we couldn't avoid. "Do you realize I will be in my forties by the time he gets out?" Claire said. "I wonder where I will be?"

I corrected her, "Don't you mean; we will be?" I said jokingly.

Her eyes turned wide. "Wow, Travis. Are we talking about a long-term relationship here?"

"Well yeah, aren't you? It's no fling for me, you know. I'm hoping by the time the monster gets out of prison, we will be in a family home somewhere in the suburbs with a couple of toddlers running around."

"You want kids with me?" she replied with a high pitch.

Her question confused me. She seemed shocked that I thought about kids. I know we've never discussed where our relationship was going, but I've pictured us as possibly married and parents someday. Had I been misreading Claire? Was I just a fling to her? Or was I moving too fast?

I shrugged my shoulders. Her parents remained quiet during the conversation that erupted between Claire and me. "Well yeah, I want kids, and yes, I want them with you." I gave her a nervous smile. Unsure of her reply. "Don't you?"

She avoided eye contact with me, which worried me. She patted my thigh and glanced at me. "We'll discuss it at home," she said with a forced smile.

Claire gave her mother a sharp stare. I wondered if there was something I didn't know. Claire then looked my way and quickly changed the subject. "Hey, are you going to tell Sabela that Davin will do more time?"

I didn't need to think about my answer and replied quickly. "No!"

Claire looked surprised. "You're not? Why?"

Well, I think it needs to come from a reputable person. A family member. Like you or your parents. If it comes from me, she may think it's here-say."

Abigale spoke with an edge to her voice. "Well, we hardly know her. We only met her twice when she lived with Davin, and it was for more than half-hour each time."

"And she hasn't seen me since she got fired from work. We aren't exactly close friends, you know," Claire said with an edge. It was clear she didn't want to be the one to tell Sabela.

"Well, that may change," I said with a smirk.

"What's that supposed to mean?" Claire asked, with her eyes narrowed.

"After she found out we were dating, she mentioned that after the dust settles, she'd like to invite us over for dinner. That would be a good time to tell her." I replied.

Claire released a loud, cracked laugh. "Oh, that would make the dinner go over well. I am the sister of the man who tried to rape her. I've already lost a few brownie points for that one. Do you honestly think she wants to talk to me? She probably only invited us to be nice to you."

I didn't join her in her laughter. "Look, she needs to know. We'll see how the evening progresses, and hopefully, we can find the right opportunity to tell her." I gave Claire's thigh an encouraging rub. "It's nothing to worry about yet. She hasn't officially invited us, and it may never happen. As you said, she might have just said it to be nice."

"Well, if it happens and I very much doubt it, I can't wait," Claire said with sarcasm.

CHAPTER 13

CLAIRE

We spent a few hours with my mom and dad at the restaurant, and I realized the selfishness I possessed. I should have been there for them and not let them cope with the heartache of their son's horrible acts on their own. I felt guilty about dad's heart attack. If they'd had my support, maybe it would have prevented him from having one.

When dad dropped us off back at our place, I promised to call him over the weekend and plan a visit soon. He smiled, which warmed my heart. It was good to see some color appear on his cheeks.

Tilly greeted us with her usual barking, but I soon quieted her down with a biscuit. I noticed Travis was quieter than usual. He removed his jacket and flung it on the back of the couch before he left the room to go to the bathroom. When he returned, he had on sweatpants and a t-shirt. He took a seat next to me on the couch as I petted Tilly,

I snuggled up to him and rubbed his thigh. "Hey, are you okay?"

He picked up a People Magazine and avoided eye contact with me. He flipped through the pages with fury. "Yeah. Why?"

"Because you're quiet and won't even look at me."

"I'm just tired," he muttered.

"Travis." I reached over and pulled the magazine away from his hands. "I know you well enough to know when something is bothering you." I placed the magazine on the table and rubbed his thigh again. "What is it, honey? You've never clammed up like this before. Talk to me."

His stare sent chills through me. His voice, stern. "I want kids someday, Claire, but I got the impression over dinner that you don't." His nostrils flared as he took in a few quick breaths. "Am I right?"

His announcement stunned me, and I wasn't ready for this conversation. I avoided his stare and lowered my eyes to the floor. My palms, sweating as I tried to swallow the lump wedged in my throat. There was an uncomfortable silence as I struggled to find my words.

"Claire?"

I lifted Tilly off my lap and placed her next to me. I rose from the couch and held clenched fists up to my mouth and paced the room. I refused to cry. I've cried too many times in the past. I shook my head as I desperately tried to fight back the tears. I heard my name again.

"Claire, what's going on?"

I looked over at Travis. My beautiful man whom I've often thought was too good for me. And now I think it's true. I couldn't be the woman that he wanted me to be. I came to terms with my future, but I didn't believe Travis ever would. I'm not prepared to tell him, but I must. Why has this come up so soon in our relationship? We've not even declared our love for each other yet, even though I knew I already did. How did we skip that step and end up talking about kids?

"Claire, talk to me," Travis repeated, but this time his voice shook.

I didn't stutter and remained calm when I spoke. I stood in the middle of the room with my arms folded under my breasts and came right out and said, "I can't have children, Travis. I'm sorry." I hung my head in shame.

Travis creased his brow. "What?" His body became limp as he fell back against the cushions. "Are you sure? How do you know?"

"Yes, I'm sure. I'm lucky if I have two periods a year. My body doesn't produce enough eggs. I have what's called Polycystic Ovary Syndrome."

Travis creased his brow again. "What the hell is that?" he asked with his eyebrow still creased.

"The doctor's described it to me as an underlying hormonal imbalance."

Travis pulled himself away from the cushions and sat with his hands hung between his legs. "What does that mean?"

Before I answered him, I hesitated. I sat on the couch next to him. My hands intertwined with his, and my heart dropped in sadness. "It means I have a hormonal imbalance and follicles, which are cysts that hang from my ovaries. These follicles are the remains of eggs that my body didn't produce." I fell silent for a minute to allow Travis to process what I had told him. "I'm infertile. I can't get pregnant." I said with a piercing stare.

Travis looked at me with a blank stare as his limp body fell back against the couch. When he spoke, his voice was flat. "How long have you known?"

"Since I turned twenty. It was a horrible year." I released a forced chuckle. "Like most of my years lately." I paused and broke into a smile, "until I met you."

He returned a smile, "Do your parents know?"

"Oh yes, they know. They supported me in their own way during that time. They reminded me of how I wasn't like other girls. I wasn't the marrying kind and more of the adventurous type that would never have time for children, anyway."

Travis's face froze. "What? That's a weird thing to say."

I nodded. "Yes, it was, but at the time it was true. I never dated, and I was always off doing something like camping, hiking, or traveling. So, I could see why they would say that."

"What about fertility drugs? Could you take them?" Travis asked, sounding hopeful.

"I've discussed it with my doctor, and the chances are very slim that they would help."

"But there is a slight possibility that they could help?" Travis asked.

"Maybe," I said in a flat tone. I didn't want to get his hopes up. "There are so many drugs and tests out there; the odds are against me; I'm not sure if it's worth it. I don't want to put myself through the disappointment if none of them work. I've accepted the fact that I will never be a mother." I took his hand. "Travis, I planned on telling you someday. I just didn't expect the conversation of kids to be coming up so soon in our relationship. I wasn't trying to hide anything from you. But after listening to you, I now know how important having children is to you." I paused. I gave him a loving smile and rubbed his hand. "Travis, you need to decide on whether you want to still be with me when there is a possibility you may never be a father."

Travis shifted in his seat and turned to face me. "Let me ask you something."

I nodded. "Okay."

"Do you want to be a mother?"

"That's a good question, and I'm going to give you my honest answer. When the doctors told me the results, my heart sank. It devastated me. I felt inadequate and yet again a failure as a woman. Other than my parents, I've not told anyone until you. I had no one in my life important enough to tell." I paused for a moment to think about my next words. "I've lived a lonely life, Travis. You are the first person I've shared it with. I came to terms with the prognosis and have learned to accept and live with it. But now you are a part of my life, and I love that you are in it." I hesitated and gave him a warm smile. "I love you, Travis. I've never said that to anyone, and yes, because of you, I want to be a mother. I want to have your children if I can. But I don't know if I'm able, and if I can't, then it will be my fault that you will never become a father."

"You love me?" Travis asked in a quiet, somber voice.

I failed at keeping my composure. My eyes were misty, and I gave him a nervous giggle. "Yes, I do." I squeezed his hand.

"Wow. This is a lot to take in."

My heart sank a notch when he didn't tell me he loved me, too, but my hopes were still high.

Maybe he's the kind of guy that didn't say it. I'm still getting to know him and discovering new things every day. Maybe I told him too soon and moved a little fast. But I had spoken from the heart. I had to be honest with him, even if it meant jeopardizing my relationship with him. My body trembled from the thought that this might break us.

"You don't have to tell me tonight. Why don't you sleep on it?" I whispered.

Travis's stare was unsettling. "I don't know what to say, Claire. Like I had said at the restaurant, I've pictured us in our suburban home as a family with kids."

His words scared me. It reminded me of the insecurities I had fought most of my life. For the first time in a long time, I felt inadequate. It terrified me that Travis may never become the father he dreams of being because of me. I thought I would be enough for him. But maybe I was wrong.

When he looked at me, my heart sank. His eyes couldn't hide the sadness he felt. The sparkle that I had grown to love was no longer visible. His face reminded me of a blank pallet, showing no emotions or color. My words were of no comfort to him. I had said what needed to be said. I couldn't feed him with false hopes for my selfish needs to coax him into staying with me. I laid the cards on the table and told him exactly how it was. I've nothing to hide.

Now all I could do was give Travis all the time he needed to process what I had revealed to him and hope he still wanted to be with me. Had he fallen in love with me as I had with him? And if he had, would it be a strong enough love to keep us together?

CHAPTER 14

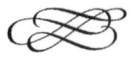

TRAVIS

When Claire told me that she was infertile, it felt like someone had kicked me in the stomach, and man did it hurt. How was I supposed to respond to that? In a matter of five minutes, all the dreams I had of our future together had been shattered. I needed time to think about how this would affect me. It tore me apart. It was my life, and what she told me was not how I had predicted it. I wanted a family more than anything.

As I turned to Claire, she looked broken and alone I thought I had known everything about her. I would have never guessed this in a million years. I couldn't imagine how devastated she felt when the doctors told her she might never have a child. As much as I dreamed about becoming a father, it had to affect a woman more so. Realizing you could never experience pregnancy and childbirth would be devastating.

I found myself lost for words and tried to make sense of this sudden blow that just happened. I didn't know how to pick up the pieces of my shattered heart. The only thing I thought of doing was to take Claire's advice. I reached over and wiped a single tear away on her cheek. "Let's go to bed. I want to hold you tight in my arms until I drift off to sleep."

She gave me a subtle smile. "Okay."

I stood up and held out my hand. She took it and pulled herself up. Her tears were plentiful and trickled down her face. "I'm so sorry," she whispered.

Guilt ripped through my body. I didn't want her to feel that way, so I pulled her into my arms. She buried her head into my chest. I cradled her and rubbed her shoulders vigorously. "Claire, it's not your fault. You didn't ask for this. My god, there is no reason for you to say you are sorry." I kissed the top of her head as she drenched my shirt with her now heavy sobs. "Come on. I'm taking you to the bed where I can hold you close to me."

Claire didn't object, so I broke away from our embrace and led her by the hand to the bedroom. We undressed in silence. Claire didn't look at me like she usually would with her seductive stare. She removed her top somberly. She looked down at the floor; she held a look of shame. I, on the other hand, couldn't take my eyes off her. She was more beautiful now; I adored her. My heart ached for her pain and for mine too.

I watched her as she sat on the edge of the bed with her back toward me. There was an upsetting silence in the room until I heard her sobs. The heart-wrenching sound tore at my heart.

"Claire?"

She buried her head into her palms and rocked her trembling body. I reached out and rested my hand on her shoulder. "Claire, please don't cry."

She gave her body a vigorous shake and stood up away from the bed. "God, I hate myself," she cried as she yanked at the belt on her jeans.

I tried to stay calm for her sake. "Claire, you are beautiful, don't say that."

She balanced on one foot as she struggled to free herself from her jeans. Her cries intensified as she spoke. "How can you say that? I can never be the woman you want me to be," she yelled.

"Come on, Claire, that's enough."

Claire spun her body to face me. Tears gushed down her flushed cheeks. Her nostrils flared, and I winced when she threw her jeans to the floor with force. Anger bled from her face. "Have you forgotten that I cannot give you a child?" Claire said in a sharp tone.

I continued to keep my calm. "Claire, come to bed. We can talk more tomorrow."

She looked down at her body and realized she was naked. She cringed while covering her breast with her hands. She sniffed back her tears. "What more is there to talk about? I can't give you what you want, Travis. So why be with me?"

I had heard enough and raised my voice. "Claire, that's enough! Stop torturing yourself. We are both exhausted. Let's sleep on it, okay?"

She didn't reply and held her head low as she slid into the bed and pulled the sheets up under her chin.

"You don't have to hide your body from me, Claire," I whispered as I reached across the bed and gently pulled the sheet down. It was just above her breasts. "Your body is beautiful. Never think it's not." I couldn't take my eyes off her as I undressed, and once in bed, I cradled her in my arms.

I breathed in the fresh scent of her hair and kissed the top of her head. She nuzzled her head in the crook of my neck. She pressed her naked body hard against mine, leaving no space. I wrapped her in my arms and held her close.

"I'm sorry," she whispered. "Please don't tell anyone about this."

"I won't, I promise." I lifted her chin and brought my face closer to hers and kissed her softly on the lips. "We will get through this and work it out."

Claire lowered her eyes away from my gaze. "I'm not so sure we can, Travis. Children are important to you."

I kissed her again. This time a little harder and longer. "Yes, they are, but so are you."

"Thank you. I needed to hear that," she said, followed by a subtle smile.

"Claire. You mean so much to me. Tonight I want to hold you close and feel the warmth of your body against mine and wake up with you still in my arms. Tomorrow is a new day, and our minds will be fresh. We'll talk more in the morning, Okay."

Claire turned her body while wrapped in my arms until we spooned one another. I circled her waist and cupped her breasts as she pressed her backside into my groin. "I like that idea," she whispered. She kissed the top of my hand. "Goodnight, Travis."

"Goodnight, Claire."

Ten minutes later, I heard the faint breathing through her nose and a delicate snore, telling me she was already asleep. I held her tight as I laid wide awake. As much as I wanted to fall asleep, I just couldn't. With my eyes wide open, I stared at the ceiling. I imagined my life without kids, and I didn't like it. I didn't want to miss out on Christmas with kids and watch them open up their presents under the tree. I wanted to watch them grow up and give them big birthday parties every year. I've dreamt of teaching them how to ride a bicycle and taking them to their first day of school. I wanted to go to their graduation and send them off to college. But most of all, I wanted to have a family and smother my wife and children with love and take care of them. And even though Claire and I have only been together a short while, I couldn't imagine my life without her either.

I felt torn. Life had thrown me a curveball, and I didn't want to choose one or the other. I wanted both, but I didn't know if that would be possible. Claire might never have children, and I kept asking myself, am I okay with that? Claire opened up to me and told me something about herself that she had never shared with anyone. I need to do the same. I must explain to her why family is so important to me.

I kept her in my arms; I leaned in and smelled the scent of her hair before gently kissing the top of her head. "Good night, Claire," I whispered.

~

I awoke before Claire and took advantage of the solitude moment by admiring her as she slept soundly. She laid on her back with a hand nestled against her cheek. The rays of the morning sun poked through the slit of the drapes, highlighting her face and hair perfectly. She looked angelic and at peace. She looked worried free, and I wanted to keep it that way, but how?

A few minutes later, she stirred. I watched closely as her eyelids fluttered, and she moved her hand over her brow. I leaned in closer before she opened her eyes. I wanted to be the first thing she saw when she woke up. A few seconds later, her eyes opened.

I kneeled in and gave her a gentle kiss on the lips. "Hey, gorgeous." I've been watching you sleep."

Claire looked dazed; she smiled in my direction. With her voice raspy, she got a few words out. "Hey. What time is it?"

"A little after seven," I announced. I gave her another kiss on the lips. It's Sunday. Why don't you relax, and I will take Tilly out to go potty? I can make us some breakfast and coffee."

She released a cute little yawn and smiled. I grinned when she stretched her arms and gave her body a sexy shake. "Okay."

Claire joined me in the kitchen thirty minutes later, wearing her bathrobe and glasses. Her hair was damp from the usual morning spray of water that she gave it.

"Hmm, that coffee smells wonderful," she said, as she stood in the middle of the room, and I handed her a fresh cup.

"It's a beautiful morning. Do you want to have breakfast out on the patio? "I asked.

"Yeah, that would be nice. Thanks."

"Okay, then. Why don't you head out there with your cup?"

Claire giggled. "You're going to serve me?"

"Yes, I am," I said with a huge grin.

"Wow! I could get used to this." She turned to Tilly, who was following her every move. "Come on, Tilly. Let's go outside."

Tilly gave a sharp bark and wagged her tail at high speed, understanding everything Claire was saying.

I wanted to do this for Claire and make her feel special. After breakfast, I intended to have a heart-to-heart talk with her and explain to her why families are so important to me. It will not be easy, but after she shared her darkest secret with me, it's only right that I share mine.

CHAPTER 15

CLAIRE

Travis was right. It was a glorious morning. Our deck had already heated by the sunrise. I took a seat, and Tilly immediately jumped into my lap like she always did and made herself comfortable.

The smell of bacon invaded my nose as I leaned back and closed my eyes and allowed the warmth from the rays of the sun to mask my face. I can't remember the last time I had sat out here. I'd forgotten how beautiful the mornings are on the deck. Travis and I needed to do this more often. I then had a disturbing thought. That's if we remain together. He still hasn't told me what he wants to do about us and our relationship. I shuddered at my next thought. Maybe he's reconsidered and doesn't want to be with me anymore. I felt scared. Perhaps that's why he hasn't said anything yet—because he's afraid to. I then thought about how long it took him to tell Jill. Was he doing all this to soften the blow when he tells me that he wants to break up?

Travis jolted me out of my upsetting mind when he appeared with two plates. "Here you go, my lady. Breakfast for one," he said with a sexy grin that I feared; I may not see much longer.

I shooed Tilly off my lap and took a plate. She didn't go far and took a seat next to my feet and waited for handouts. I turned to Travis and forced a smile while trying to shake the horrible thoughts I had been having.

Travis took a seat in the vacant chair. "Damn, it's nice out here. Why haven't we done this before?"

"I was just thinking the same thing. I used to sit out on the deck in the other unit every morning and have my coffee. I'd forgotten how refreshing it is."

"Well, I think we need to do this every day. It certainly puts a smile on my face."

He gave me hope when he mentioned doing things together after today, and I forced another smile. "Makes me smile too," I said before taking a few bites of my scrambled eggs.

As much as Travis tried to lighten the mood, I felt the tension between us, and I wanted to make light-hearted conversation to make it go away. "So, what do you want to do today?" I asked.

Travis tried to fight the uncomfortable vibes that lingered between us, and when his smile suddenly disappeared, I immediately felt a chill. I knew we had lost the battle. "Do you feel like doing anything?" he asked.

I shrugged my shoulders and let out a heavy sigh. "I don't know Travis. You tell me." I leaned back in my chair and allowed my body to go limp. I felt emotionally drained from worry. "Where do we go from here? I need to know if you still want to be with me." I closed my eyes for a second to fight back the tears. "Let's not drag this out as you did with Jill. You either want to be with me, or you don't."

Travis shied away from my stare, which worried me. He didn't give me a straight yes or no right away. Oh my god. Were my fears about to come true? Was Travis going to break up with me?

CHAPTER 16

TRAVIS

I stayed awake most of the night, listening to the voices in my head. They wouldn't shut up, but I realized what was important to me. I looked over at Claire. She couldn't hide the worry that blanketed her face. I reached over and took her hand. Her skin soft to the touch, but her hands cold as ice. I caressed them with my fingers and gave her a subtle smile before telling her my story.

"Claire, you are the most important thing to me in my life. I need you to know that. When you told me last night that you might not get pregnant, I will not lie to you; it devastated me. I've always pictured myself with a few kids. We would raise them right and smother them with love." I paused and gave her a stare with my eyes narrowed. "It's something I'd never experience growing up."

Claire creased her brow. "What? Were your parents mean to you?"

I shook my head. "No. I never knew them. They gave me up for adoption when I was born, and I spent my entire childhood until I was eighteen in and out of foster homes, and for six months when I was fourteen, I was placed me in a juvenile detention center."

Claire's eyes grew wider as she covered her gaped mouth with her free hand. "Oh my god, Travis, I'm so sorry. I guess we both had a secret to tell one another." She broke into a half-smile. "So, I guess that's why family is so important to you because you've never had one."

I nodded. "Yes, it is. Growing up, I never felt wanted. I was a punk kid with an attitude, and no one could handle me. At twelve, I smoked cigarettes, shoplifted, and even dabbled with alcohol. They placed me in detention for vandalism and shoplifting. I lived in sixteen foster homes, and the longest time I spent at one was just under a year. I don't know who my parents are or if I have any brothers or sisters. And you know what sucks is that I've never had the privilege of calling someone mom or dad. That may sound silly, but those two words give you a sense of belonging. Just like Grandpa and Grandma, which I've never said to anyone either."

Claire squeezed my hands and looked at me with pity in her eyes. "Travis, I'm so sorry. I couldn't imagine growing up with no parents." Suddenly I could tell she understood me. She stiffened her body slightly and tilted her head. "Wait. That's why you were adamant about me making up with my parents. Isn't it? Because I was destroying what you never had."

I gave her a subtle smile and nodded again. "Yep. When you first told me I wanted to say something back then, but I had only just met you. When they showed up here, I just had to do something."

She took in a deep breath and fell back against the chair and let go of my hand. "Oh my god. And you did." She retook my hand and gave it a hard squeeze. "Thank you. If it wasn't for you, I would have sent them on their way and would probably still not be speaking to them."

"I couldn't stand to see the hurt in all of your eyes. You were hurting. Your parents were hurting, but none of you knew how to fix it. It took someone like me on the outside with no emotions clouding my mind to bring you guys back together." I changed my tone to a more serious manner and gave her a hard stare. "Claire, never abandon your parents again. We all make mistakes but cherish what you have while they are here because when they die, you will miss them. I envy you and would give anything to experience what you have. It's one reason I dream about being a dad someday. I want to give a child or two what I never had."

Claire's sadness appeared on her face again. "So, where does that leave us?" she asked with fear seeping through her words.

I took a deep breath. "I did a lot of thinking last night and thought a lot about my childhood. All I ever wanted was a family to take me in and love me like I was their own. But I was a messed up kid that I wouldn't allow anyone in. I never understood that until last night. If I had been a well-behaved kid, I could have grown up with only one set of foster parents that would probably have adopted me and loved and raised me as if I were their own. But as arrogant as I was, I didn't give myself or the families a chance. If we can't have our own, then I would be perfectly happy saving another kid from foster care and prevent them from going through what I experienced."

Claire lifted her shoulders with a look of hope. "So, what are you saying?"

I gave her my biggest smile since last night. "I'm saying that I don't want to spend my life with anyone else but you. I've never had a fulfilling relationship or felt so at ease with anyone before. I know I can tell you anything, be it good or bad." I squeezed her hand. "I love you, Claire, and no matter what, if we have our own kids or adopt, I want you to be their mom."

Claire couldn't hold back her tears, and before I said any more, she left her seat in a mad dash and fell into my lap. She wrapped her arms tightly around my neck. "Oh, Travis, you don't know how happy you've just made. I've been so scared, thinking you didn't want to be with me. I love you so much," she said between her tears of happiness. "Kiss me."

I held her head between my palms and devoured her lips as her salty tears dripped on my face. We kissed passionately, smothering each other. We held each other tight as we expressed our love for each other between gasps of air. "I love you so frigging much, Claire. I'll never leave you," I said and stole another passionate kiss.

"And I'll never leave you, Travis. You make me so happy," Her chest heaved as she spoke between her sobbing. "Someday, we will have a family. Adopted or our own."

I brushed her hair away from her face and tilted her chin until she looked into my eyes. "I know we will, sweetheart." I gave her a massive smile. "You know something?"

"What?" Claire replied.

"If it turns out you can get pregnant, I think I would still like to foster a few kids and save them from the heartache of what I went through." I smiled again. "What do you say? Are you up to having a large family?"

Claire gave me a smile that instantly put me at ease. "I think it's a brilliant idea." She nestled her head in the crook of my neck. "You will be a wonderful dad, Travis. You have so much love inside of you to give to a child."

I cradled my arm around her shoulder and pulled her in close. "We will be great parents. We'll get through this together and make the right decisions when the time comes."

Claire looked up and smiled. "I know we will."

I shifted in my seat and kissed her again on the lips. "In the meantime, let's go back to bed. I want to spend the rest of the morning making love to you over and over again."

Claire pulled herself out of my lap and stood. "You read my mind." She took my hand and pulled me out of my seat.

CHAPTER 17

CLAIRE

When Travis told me his story, it shocked me, but it brought us closer together. After what I revealed to him the night before, my painful truths and his devastating childhood. Something happened between us in those twelve hours. We shared raw emotions, and it created a heavy bond between us. All of my fears and insecurities that had flooded my head had vanished. It left warmth and gratitude for having this man in my life. I never thought I could love a man so deeply as I do Travis. My heart reminded me of how wrong I had been. It was full, and I wanted to burst with joy.

He led me into the bedroom, and as promised, he made love to me all morning. It was beyond beautiful. He devoured every inch of my body with heated sensual kisses, as I did with him. We filled our lungs with each other's scents and entangled our bodies until we became one. He seduced me with his dreamy eyes. His husky voice declared his love for me repeatedly. We made love with our eyes open, lost in each other's gaze, memorized by what we had. When we came the first time, we came together, holding one another tight, not wanting to let go. He screamed my name, and I yelled his name. Our bodies were saturated with sweat. Fatigue overwhelmed us, but we craved each other more. I gave Travis everything I had to give that morning, my mind, my body, and my heart. He devoured me completely, and I grasped him until we laid lifeless in each other's arms, gasping for air. My hair drenched in sweat. I rested it on his moist chest and listened to his heart pound in my ear. After four intense orgasms, the bed had become a tangled mess.

Our chests heaved as we brought ourselves back down to earth. Our breathing turned loud and shallow. We smiled happily at one another.

"Damn, that was fucking amazing," Travis said as he caught his breath. "I've never felt so in tune before with someone while making love." He pulled me in closer and gave me a tight squeeze. "That was the real deal, Claire. I completely lost myself with you. It was almost like I was floating. That was unreal."

I chuckled at his confession but understood because I felt the same way. I had no words to describe what I had experienced with Travis. He was right; it was real, and it was raw. The best part about it, it was ours to treasure. I propped myself up on my elbows and met his lips with mine. "Thank you for seeing something in me that I never saw." I kissed him again; I smothered his lips with mine. He collapsed beneath me and let his head fall into the softness of the pillow and cupped the back of my head with his palms. For the next few minutes, we kissed hard and passionate as our heads became lighter, and our bodies became limp.

When our kiss ended, Travis looked at me and whispered, "You are every man's dream, Claire. You've shown me what genuine love truly feels like. And for that, I thank you."

I gave him a loving smile and then asked him something that I needed to know. "Can I ask you something?" I said as I propped my head on my arm for support.

Travis rolled his body and mirrored me by supporting his head with his arm too. "Sure. After our amazing morning, you can ask me anything."

My tone turned serious. "Have you ever thought about looking for your birth parents? Do you know why they gave you up?"

Travis took in a deep breath. "Those are some big questions, and the short answer is no. I never wanted to look for them, and the only thing I know is that the woman that gave birth to me was fifteen. I'm sure she couldn't have been married. She was just a kid herself."

"Can I ask why you never thought about looking for them? And tell me to shut up if I'm being too nosey."

Travis traced the surface of my nose and laughed. "No, it's fine. The reason I don't want to find them is that more than likely, I had been a mistake. I mean, who plans to have a child at fifteen and besides almost thirty years have passed. I'm not going to start looking now."

"Why not?" I asked.

Travis shrugged his shoulders and searched for his words. "Because they are not someone I could ever call mom or—they certainly haven't earned the title. They hold no purpose in my life. And it's clear they haven't tried looking for me."

"Don't you think if your mother was so young when she had you that her parents probably forced her to give you up? What about your dad? Do you know anything about him?"

Travis shook his head. "No, I don't."

"So who told you that your mom was fifteen?"

"I don't remember her name. She was one of my foster parents. One of her biological sons was a few years older than me. I was around eight years old. He always called me nasty names and would tell me I was weird because I didn't have a mom. Anyway, his mom heard him, and she had pulled me aside and explained to me that I had a mother, but she had me when she was only fifteen, and that was too young to take care of a baby."

My heart ached for Travis. I couldn't imagine going through

life not knowing who my parents were. "So, you have no idea if your parents were together when you were born?"

"Nope." Travis sat up and rested his head on the pillow. He took my hand and kissed it. "The way I look at it Claire, they gave me up, and they should be the ones to do the footwork if they want me to be a part of their lives. As far as I know, they've not done that. I don't see anyone knocking at my door or writing to me, and I'm not going to spend my time looking for someone that may not want me in their life."

I squeezed Travis's hand. "Maybe they don't know how or where to begin. I know I wouldn't." I gave him a hard stare. "I'm only going to put this out there. We don't have to do anything if you don't want to, but if your mother is still alive, she would only be forty-five. That's still young, Travis. There would still be plenty of time for you two to get to know each other and maybe find out about your dad if she is no longer with him."

Travis shook his head from side to side. "Oh, I don't know, Claire. I don't think that would be a good idea."

The fact that Travis didn't give me a direct no, led me to think he wasn't totally against the idea. "Travis, you shared with me how important family is to you. You reconnected me with my parents. If there is a remote chance that you could find yours, I want to help you. I just want you to know that, okay? I only ask that you think about it."

Travis smiled. "You would do that for me?"

I gave him a snarky grin. "We would do it together. But only if you want to."

He kissed the top of my head. "Okay."

I rested my head on his chest, and together we held each other close for a while in silence.

I'm not sure how long we laid naked nestled in each other's arms. I think I drifted off to sleep when the sound of Tilly's bark on the other side of the door alerted me. I didn't want to move and procrastinated. "Oh, Tilly wants to go out," I mumbled.

Travis yawned. "Huh?"

"Oh, you fell asleep too," I giggled.

"I guess so. You wore me out, woman. What did you say?"

I sat up and laughed at his delirious state. "I said Tilly needs to go out. Let's get dressed and take her for a nice long walk. She's been cooped up while we've been fooling around for the past few hours."

We took Tilly for an extended walk through the park across the street. It was a gorgeous afternoon with perfect temperatures and a slight breeze. Travis held the leash and draped his arm over my shoulder with his free hand. Being a good six inches shorter than him, I could rest my head on his chest and lock my arms around his waist. Our words were few, but our emotions were high. We were both still in awe of knowing what we had was something most people only dream of. Occasionally we needed to stop in our steps and just gaze at each other in silence. A satisfactory smile would break out between us, followed by a slow sensual kiss. And even though the park was busy with other dog walkers and kids playing, it felt like we were the only ones there.

We continued to walk for another hour locked in each other's embrace, oblivious to the rest of the word until Travis stopped again and combed his fingers through my hair, brushing it away from my face. "Are you ready to go back home?" he asked.

I took his hand and brought it to my lips. "Sure."

He smiled. "Do you know what I'd like to do when we get back."

"No. What?"

He swept my hair back some more. "I want to spend the rest of the day in bed with you. I want a repeat of this morning," he laughed.

I laughed at his request. "You're good at reading my mind. I couldn't think of a better way to spend the afternoon."

"And evening." Travis chuckled before he leaned in and kissed me again.

CHAPTER 18

TRAVIS

Over the next month, I continued to work with Slater and Sabela at Eve's house. They paid me well, and I insisted on paying for everything with Claire at home. Claire protested at first, but she realized how important it was for me to be the man of the household. I guess I'm old-fashioned. I've always been the main provider in a relationship, and Claire understood that. Especially when I suggested she bank her check for our future because I wouldn't be making this kind of money all the time.

For the first time in my life, I had a sense of belonging, and it felt fantastic. My relationship with Claire went deeper than just a physical attraction, unlike others I have had. On weekends we have gone camping a few times, and when we couldn't get away, then we'd go for day hikes. We've spent the evening playing board games and reading books to each other. I love how we interacted with each other, and it's not all about sex. We've not ventured back to the nude beach yet because of our close call with Sabela and Slater, but it's still on our list of adventures to do.

Claire has as usual kept to herself at work and hasn't discussed her life outside of it, which she'd never done, anyway. But it seems the urgency to tell Jill about us has lifted as more time has gone by. From what Claire had told me, Sadie, the new girl at the office, was now Jill's new best friend and roommate. Claire, frequently, overheard them giggling and whispering in the lobby about dates they've had with guys and upcoming parties they were going to. So it seemed clear that Jill had moved on just like me.

I knew; eventually, she will find out about Claire and me. We were okay with that. We no longer fear Jill's reaction or care what she thinks. I've even mentioned to Claire that it's about time I come to her work and take her out for lunch. Surprisingly, she didn't object. So I can see that happening soon.

I had hoped to surprise Claire this week by going to her work unannounced and take her somewhere, but Slater had called me with some unbelievable and also devastating news that I'm still trying to wrap my head around. I had just gotten to the job site when my phone rang.

"Hey, Travis, it's Slater."

I sensed by the flat tone of his voice that something was wrong. He wasn't his usual upbeat self. "Hey. Everything okay?"

There was a moment of silence, and then I heard Slater take a deep breath before he spoke. "No, not really. Eve is dead."

I gasped and had to steady my feet. My knees felt weak, and I feared I might fall, and I let my body plop on to the front step outside the house, "What?"

Slater's voice sounded broken. "She's dead, man. She had brain cancer and didn't tell anyone. Only her family knew. She left me a letter. I just found out."

I shook my head in disbelief and raked my hand through my hair, "Jesus man. We knew she was hiding something. But damn, I never imagined anything like this. I'm so sorry."

"Thanks, I still can't believe it. I honestly don't know how to react. When she showed up here and asked me to work for her, I was mean to her. After the way she had left me, I just didn't trust her." Slater explained.

"Well, I'd probably be the same way. Don't beat yourself up, man. You were just protecting yourself. You weren't going to allow her to hurt you again like she did when she walked out on you, and you came home to a note."

"Yeah, I know. Why didn't she tell me? Don't you think I had a right to know? And that's not the half of it."

"You mean there's more?"

Slater took another deep breath. "Scottie is my son. She kept that from me too."

Relieved I was sitting down, my jaw dropped, and my eyes bulged. "Oh my god. You are Scottie's dad. How are you handling that? Wow!"

"I just found all this out. It's all still sinking in; I can't believe I am a dad. Eve had this entire thing planned out up to her death. It's in the letter she'd left behind. I'm sad for her. She was so young, and Scottie will grow up not knowing his mother."

I kept my thoughts to myself, but Slater's words took me back to my motherless childhood, and my heart ached for Scottie. "I'm sure Sabela will be a wonderful mom to him. Oh, wait. What does she think about all this? She's going to have to raise a child that is not hers."

"Sabela has been amazing. She wants to be Scottie's mom. I know she will raise him like he is her own. I just hope he will be okay coming home with us. He doesn't know us, and I'm scared to death how he will react. We're going to meet him for the first time and tell him that he will live with us. He's only four years old. That poor child." Slater struggled to find his word. "Why couldn't Eve be upfront with me when she knew she was dying? God. I'm so sorry she had to go through it alone. Things would have been so much easier if she'd had just told me."

"I guess it just wasn't Eve's nature. She doesn't sound like someone who liked to talk. Leaving letters seems to be her MO. She split up with you through a letter and now this."

Slater didn't reply.

"Hey man, if there's anything I can do. Let me know. Okay?"

"Yeah, there is. It's why I called. Sabela and I are leaving this afternoon to pick up Scottie. We're going to swing by and pick up some of his things. And if you're okay with it, I'd like to leave you in charge. We want to take some time off so we can be with Scottie."

"Sure, no problem, man. Take all the time you need."

"Thanks, I appreciate it. Listen, I need to get going. Call me if you need anything."

"I will. And hey, Slater."

"Yeah."

"Scottie will be fine. Just give him some time."

"I will. I'll talk to you soon. Bye."

After I had hung up the phone I stared off into the distance for a while. Numbed by the sudden news of Eve's death and that Slater was Scottie's dad. I just couldn't believe it.

I'm not going to lie; I felt a twinge of jealousy when Slater told me he was a dad. Going home and telling Claire the news wasn't easy. We hadn't bought up the subject on her infertility again. We had been so busy enjoying each other that we avoided the issue. But I heard the pride in Slater's voice when he told me; it stirred up raw emotions.

"Wow. Slater is a dad," Claire said. I told her the whole story that had unfolded after Eve's death, which was a shock to all of us. Claire flopped onto the couch like a rag-doll and welcomed Tilly into her lap. She shook her head. "I can't believe Eve kept such a secret from Slater. All this time, she knew she was dying from a brain tumor and tracked down Slater, who is Scottie's real father, so that Slater could raise him."

I nodded as I sat next to her and draped my arm over her shoulder. "Yep, and they've left me in charge to finish the job so they can spend some time with him."

Claire rubbed my thigh. "Are you okay?" she asked.

I had tried to deny what I was feeling. "Yeah, why?"

But Claire knew me too well and wasn't buying it. "Come on, Travis. Be honest with me. Doesn't it sting it little that Slater has a son? It does for me."

I nodded. "Yeah, it does. Slater's voice was filled with pride when he told me on the phone." I gave a heavy sigh. "I would love to know how that feels."

"I hope someday we can tell our friend we are going to be parents," Claire confessed.

I leaned in and kissed her gently on the cheek. "I hope so too."

Slater had called me every day on the job, checking on the progress, but most of the conversation was about his son and that the shock factor was still an issue.

"I have to keep pinching myself that I'm a dad," he said yesterday morning. "Wait till you have a kid, Travis. It's an unbelievable feeling."

His words stung, and I'm glad he couldn't see my face when my smile vanished.

Today was no exception. Slater had called early this morning and said he would stop by the job later in the day to see how everything was going. The job was winding down, and we'd hoped to have it completed within the next two weeks. He hadn't gone into details on what he wanted to do with the house now that it was his. He and Sabela were going over their options.

Later in the afternoon, Slater pulled into the driveway as I grabbed some paint from the garage. I hadn't seen him in a while, but I sure noticed a difference in him. When he stepped out of the truck, he wore an enormous smile, and his entire mannerism and stride just radiated happiness. I set down the two cans of paint I was carrying and approached him with my arm extended and shook his hand. "Hey, man. It's good to see," I said as I gripped his shoulder with my other hand.

As we stood there face to face, I tried desperately to block the images I had of him naked at the beach. It haunted me for the first few minutes whenever I saw Slater now.

Slater's beamed an enormous smile. "Hey, Travis. It's good to see you too."

I gave him a forced smile. "Congratulations again on suddenly becoming a dad. But man, I still can't believe Eve kept it all from you. The whole situation is so sad. She was holding quite a few secrets."

For the first time, Slater lost his smile. "Yeah, I wished she's been upfront with me from the beginning. I can't help but feel sorry for her. She could never speak the truth about anything. I always had to figure out what was going on in her head. But she did do the right thing by making sure I got Scottie. She went about it all wrong. But that was Eve."

I nodded. "So how is Sabela enjoying being a new mom?"

Slater's smile returned. "Oh, man, she's a natural. Scottie has taken to her so well. She spends all her time with him. They bake, they read stories. She brought him a tricycle just last week, and she takes him around the block. We both enjoy taking him to the park almost every day." He paused for a second to bring his excitement down a notch. "And do you know what Sabela and I do every night after we've tucked him into bed?"

"No, what?" I asked.

"We grab Scottie's stools, sit by his bed, and watch him sleep. Sometimes it will be for over an hour. I look at his innocent little face and his eyelids flickering, and I can't believe he is ours. There is no greater love you give to your son." He nudged my arm with his forearm. "You wait, Travis. You'll see."

At that moment, I shifted my stare away and nodded.

Slater placed his hands in his front pockets and took a step back. "You know Sabela, and I have been talking, and we'd love for you and Claire to meet Scottie."

My face froze. "You and Sabela want me and Claire to meet Scottie. Is that what you said?'

Slater flashed a smile. "Yes, Travis, both of you. We want to have you over for dinner some night."

I gave my head a quick shake in disbelief. "And Sabela is okay with Claire coming?"

"Yes. In fact, it was her idea."

I was shocked by what I heard. "You're kidding. I remember her mentioning it when she first found out about Claire and me, but I didn't think she was serious." I gave Slater a hard stare. "Honestly, man, what do you think about it? Are we going to witness a catfight over dinner?" I joked.

Slater cracked a laugh. "I think the girls will behave. After all, Scottie will be at the table too, you know."

"Oh yeah. Shit. I keep forgetting you're a dad. Sorry, bro."

He didn't acknowledge my apology and kept on talking. "After what you said about Claire that she was only the sister of the man that tried to rape her, it opened up not only Sabela's eyes but mine too. We treated Claire unfairly. You were right, and we owe you both an apology."

I admired his honesty. "Well, thanks, man. I appreciate it. I think it's a good idea that we get together. I've missed those days."

"Me, too," Slater said as he gave my arm another nudge.

"I'm just not sure how Claire will react to the idea,"

"Well, I hope she will come. We were thinking this Saturday, and you can tell her we won't bite." Slater chuckled.

I laughed. "I'll do my best, but I can't promise anything. Claire is an independent woman, and if she doesn't want to do something, she has no problem letting me know." I bent down and picked up the two cans of paint. "Now, come on, let me show what we've done in the house."

We spent the next few hours walking through the house, admiring our work, and going over the remaining tasks.

"So, do you have any idea what you are going to do with this place once it's finished?" I asked.

Slater glanced around the entranceway where we stood. "I'm not sure. Maybe you can help me decide over dinner."

"Me? Well, you could always move in. It is yours, you know?"

"Nah. We could never live here. It's not us. It's too big and too rich for my taste."

"It's a shame. We have done so much work to make it perfect for Scottie. Maybe you'll have second thoughts.

"No. This house already has a sad history in the short time Eve lived here. I think it's best we start fresh in a new place. I have a few ideas for this place. I'll run them by you over dinner. I think Eve would have approved.".

"Maybe Sabela and Claire can come up with some fresh ideas," I suggested, as we locked up the house and headed back to our trucks.

"That's a good idea. Four heads are better than one." Slater laughed. He looked at his watch. "Speaking of which, we are taking Scottie to the movies. I have to run. Call me tomorrow, okay."

"I sure will."

After Slater had left, I checked my phone and saw it was 4'o'clock. Slater surprised me with his dinner invitation, but I also admired how he and Sabela were willing to make amends and start fresh with Claire. It took a lot of class to do that, and those two certainly had enough of it. If Claire agreed to go on Saturday, I was looking forward to recapturing the friendship we had before. But Slater's actions also made me realize that I needed to stop beating around the bush and come clean with someone so Claire and I can finally move forward and be the power couple we both want to be.

I rechecked my phone. I still had time to take care of the one thing that hung over our heads since the day I moved in with Claire. I felt good about my sudden change of heart thanks to Slater. I hopped into my truck. "Well, no time like the present," I uttered. I backed out of the driveway and sped down the street, eager to beat the clock; I had at least a thirty-minute drive ahead.

CHAPTER 19

CLAIRE

I couldn't wait until five o'clock rolled around. After being on my feet most of the day, they were killing me by four. I wanted to be lying on my couch with my naked feet in Travis's lap, watching a movie as he gave me one of his awesome foot massages. It had become a regular thing and something I looked forward to every night. I loved how he spoiled me. Tonight I plan on making him a special dinner because he does so much for me, and I want to do something for him in return.

At a little after four-thirty, I took what I hoped would be the last x-ray of the day, but before shutting down the machine, I headed out to the reception area to check with Jill. We didn't speak much to each other. It's always been that way. She worked in the front, and I in the back in my little room. Since hiring Sadie, lunches had become easier too. She no longer hung out in the break room. Instead, she and Sadie ate out every day. I walked out into the lobby and noticed the waiting area was empty.

"Any more patients scheduled?" I hollered across the room to Jill.

"No. That's it." Jill replied.

I turned around and left to shut down the x-ray machine when I saw a truck pull into the parking lot. Jill saw it too and peered over her screen.

"Who the hell is that? We're closing in fifteen minutes." She shook her head. "They will have to come back tomorrow." And then she spoke again. "Oh, shit!"

Jill had a better view than from where I stood, and I couldn't see what caused her to cuss. "What?" I said as I began walking to the front desk to get a better view.

"It's frigging, Travis."

I almost tripped from her words and couldn't hide the horror in my voice as I shrieked. "What!"

Jill leaned back in her chair and folded her arms. "This may not be pretty. I knew he'd come running back. Well, have I got news for him. I'm having too much fun dating again. There's no way I'm going back to him."

I didn't respond to her almighty speech. I was too busy staring out the window with a gigantic knot in my throat. My heart pounded in my chest. "What the hell is he doing here?" I whispered under my breath.

Jill glanced my way. "What did you say?"

"Er, nothing," I tried to swallow. I watched as Travis stepped out of his truck, closed the door, and headed our way.

Jill let out a cocky laugh. "I can't believe he would come to my work and put me on the spot like this. Wait till I tell Sadie." She looked over her shoulder. "Where is she anyway? I bet she'd loved to see this."

At that moment, I wanted to run the other way through the back doors and hide. I couldn't believe Travis was here. What was he doing? Why hadn't he called me first? Or had he? In a state of panic, I reached into the side pocket of my pants and pulled out my phone. I checked for missed calls. There were none. My eyes darted to the door once more. Travis now had his hand on the handle and pulled it open. I stood frozen to my spot and held my breath.

"What are you doing here?" Jill snarled before he spoke.

"Hi, Jill." Well, It's good to see you too." Travis said with sarcasm oozing from his voice.

I remained silent as they exchanged words.

"I don't want a scene, Travis," Jill said as she stood up and folded her arms.

Travis shook his head and looked my way. He threw me a smile and a sexy wink. I quickly shied away to avoid being caught, giving him a flirtatious smile. But Travis wasn't discreet. I watched with horror as he walked towards me while still wearing his beautiful smile. I didn't know where to look. I certainly didn't know what to do or say.

Jill placed her hands on her hips. "Where are you going? I am talking to you," she snapped.

Travis ignored her and shooed her off with his arms. He flashed me an even bigger smile and whispered. "Hi."

I whispered back while still frozen to my spot. "What are you doing?"

This time he talked in a normal tone and reached out for my hand. "Something that I should have done a long time ago."

I took his hand and followed his lead while avoiding eye contact with Jill.

Jill kept her hands on her hips and creased her brow. "What's going on?" she asked.

Travis led me over to the front desk and stood across from Jill with the desk between us. He gave me a reassuring smile and wrapped his arm over my shoulder before he spoke.

"Jill, there won't be a scene unless you want to start one, but I think it's time you should know that Claire and I are dating."

"What!" Jill shrieked. "Are you effing kidding me?"

Travis shook his head. "No, I'm not kidding." He looked into my eyes and flashed me another gorgeous smile.

This time I smiled back and took his hand.

"I know we should have told you a long time ago, and I apologize, but honestly, we didn't know how."

Jill's jaw dropped, and her eyes became wide. She gave me a stare and then Travis. "You and Claire are an item? How long has this been going on?" Suddenly she put two and two together and raised a hand to her brow. "Wait! Is this why you broke up with me? Because of her?" She snarled with a curled lip.

"Now wait just a minute, Jill. We both had agreed that we were over long before we split up. But yes, I was seeing Claire at that time."

Jill's eyes narrowed as she stared me down and gave me a piercing look when she spoke. "And you hid this from me the whole time. How could you?" she shrieked. "He was my boyfriend, and you've come here every day to work and not said a damn thing."

Travis butted in before I replied. "We didn't plan on this happening, but it did. I feel bad that I didn't tell you sooner, but I'm telling you now. I want us all to be adults about this and try to get along. I know you've moved on, Jill. Well, so have I, and you need to accept that." Travis rubbed my shoulder and pulled me in closer. "You may work with Claire. But you don't know her. You've never given her a chance or taken the time to find out who she is. How was she supposed to tell you when you guys hardly speak to each other?"

Jill folded her arms and rolled her eyes. "Well, it's not my fault she hides in that little room all day."

I pulled away from Travis's hold. "Will you guys stop talking like I'm not even here?" I snapped and narrowed my eyes at Jill. "Maybe it was wrong of me not to say anything to you. Trust me, there were many times I wanted to, but in all honesty, like Travis said, I didn't know how." I leaned over the counter and hissed my words. "Yes, I hide in my little room all day, but it's far better than the chilled cold shoulder I get from you every time I come out here."

"What's that's supposed to mean?" Jill contested.

"You know damn well what it means. You've never been friendly toward me or invited me out to dinner or drinks after work. Why is that Jill? Is it because I wear glasses and I'm too square for you?"

Travis took my arm. "Okay, that's enough."

I shook my arm and gave Travis a hard stare. "Let me finish!" I turned to face Jill. "You acted surprised and disgusted that Travis and I are dating. Don't you think I'm good enough for him?"

Jill raised her voice. "I never said that."

"No, but that's what you meant." My nostrils flared. "Let me tell you something, Jill. Travis was too good for you. Now I'm not going to stand here and be ridiculed by someone who doesn't even know me. I love Travis, and I refuse to apologize for that. You either accept it, or you don't. I honestly don't care. The only thing I'll apologize for is not telling you sooner."

Travis took my hand. "I'm the one at fault here. It's never been Claire's responsibility to tell you, Jill. And yes, I fucked up by not telling you sooner."

Jill curled her lip and spat out her words. "Yes, Travis, I had a right to know. You should have told me the truth about why you broke up with me. It was because of her."

Travis released a sarcastic laugh. "Now you and I both know that is not the reason. We were over months before I even started seeing Claire, so don't even say that. And I never told you about her then because I was afraid you would have made things difficult for her here at work."

"Well, this is weird, Travis. I do have to work with her, and she's now dating my ex-boyfriend." Jill snarled.

"She has a name, Jill. Yes, you work together. But it's not like you're best friends, for god's sake. Why should that matter? Claire has worked just fine for the past few months. Why can't you? Or are you going to be childish about this and make it bigger than it is?'

Jill softened her tone a notch. "Look, Travis, this is quite a shock, okay. Give me some time to get used to the idea. I didn't think Claire was your type." She turned to me and forced a tiny smile. "No offense, Claire. But you and I are like night and day."

Travis spat out his next words. "And what is that supposed to mean, Jill? I lived with you for over four years, and you never got to know me. Just like you've worked with Claire, and you still don't know her. You don't know my type and nor did I until I met Claire." Travis raised his voice. "I wanted to come clean with you, and I have. I'm sorry I screwed up and waited, but now you know. I hope someday you can be happy for us, and I hope you find *your type* soon because when you do, I'll be happy for you and who knows, maybe we can all be friends again."

Travis broke away and took my hand. "Come on, Claire. I'm done here."

I nodded and turned to Jill. My lips narrowed. "I too hope someday you can accept that Travis and I are a couple and not think about yourself all the time. If you make our workplace an uncomfortable environment, there's nothing I can do about that, but I'll handle it just fine."

"I just need some time, okay," Jill said in a flat tone. She looked over her shoulder. "Look, I'm going to go find Sadie. We're supposed to have some drinks after work, and I really need one now. I'll talk to you later."

I watched as she walked through the back door and left us standing alone, holding hands.

Travis squeezed my hand. "How are you doing? Are you okay?"

"Yeah, I'm fine."

He lowered his head and looked into my eyes. "You're not mad at me for coming here without telling you, are you?."

I shook my head and chuckled. "No, not at all. In fact, I'm relieved. If you had told me, I would have somehow talked you out of it. It's finally out in the open, and we can stop hiding." I gave him a loving smile. "So, thank you."

Travis smiled and kissed me. "You're welcome. Now come on, let's get out of here."

Outside in the parking lot, he took me in his arms and gave me a long sensual kiss. "I want to take you out for dinner to celebrate my coming clean moment. It feels so frigging good. Why did I wait so long?"

"I was planning on making you a nice home-cooked meal because you've been so amazing lately, but dinner at a restaurant does sound much better, I have to admit," I said as I embraced the strength of his hold.

Travis swayed me in his arms from side-to-side and planted another kiss on my lips. "Wait, a minute. A cozy dinner at home, I like that idea too," he said, followed by a smirk. "But I don't want you to slave over a hot stove after working all day. Come on; we're going out to eat," he insisted.

I didn't argue and told him I would follow him to the restaurant so we wouldn't have to come back for my car. He agreed, and in forty minutes, we were at the seafood shack on the beach, sitting outside on the deck, enjoying a glass of white wine. It was a glorious evening with a slight breeze in the air. I could hear the waves crashing against the shore in the distance, and the sky changed colors from red to orange as the sunset over the ocean.

I hadn't asked Travis about his sudden change of heart on telling Jill about us. I could tell he didn't want to stick around in the parking lot and have a conversation, but it blew me away by his unannounced visit. I was happy that everything was now out in the open, but; I had to return to work tomorrow and face Jill. How the hell was that going to be, I wondered. My anxiety level had peaked again.

"So why did you tell Jill?" I asked after taking a sip of wine.

Travis leaned back and spanned his arms across the back of the booth. He looked at me with a satisfactory smile. "It was a spur-of-the-moment thing, and I acted on it."

"I'd say." I laughed.

"It was after I saw Slater." He shook his head. "Oh, I almost forgot. There's something else I have to tell you. It's what gave me the idea to tell Jill."

"Oh, god. Is this going to be another surprise?"

Travis was silent for a moment, and then he leaned forward and took a deep breath. "Slater and Sabela have invited us over for dinner this weekend. They want us to meet Scottie."

My jaw dropped, and my eyes felt like they might pop out of my head. "What? You're kidding."

Travis shook his head. "Nope. I'm not kidding."

"Are you sure it's not just you that they invited? We know damn well how Sabela feels about me."

"Slater specifically told both of us, and he even said that he and Sabela had discussed it and that they owe you an apology."

I gasped. "Me? Why?"

"Because they realized after I had pointed it out to them that you are not responsible for Davin's crimes. And you are an innocent victim. They finally understood, and I guess they want to make things right between us." He gave me one of his cute smiles. "That's when I got the idea that I should come clean with Jill, and before I gave it a second thought, I jumped in my truck, and well, you know the rest. I think it's decent of them, don't you?"

I was stunned by what Travis had told me. Sabela and I had never been close, but the fact that she wanted to try a friendship with me told me a lot about her. And Slater too, for that matter. I suddenly had a tremendous amount of admiration for them. Not only were they willing to admit their faults, but they also wanted to fix them too. I could see how their act inspired Travis to come clean with Jill. How could I possibly not accept their invitation? I needed to follow their example and quit living in the past. I wasn't expecting to be their next best friend, but this was a positive move in the right direction.

I smiled across the table at Travis, who had waited patiently for my answer. "Yes, I'll go."

Travis's eyes became wide. "You will?" he said and then shook his head. "Wow. I wasn't expecting that."

I laughed. "I wasn't either when you first asked me. But it's the right thing to do. Sabela and Slater are putting themselves out on a limb, and I should do the same." I threw him another smile. "I'll even bake a cake for the occasion. Call it a peace offering."

"I like that idea. Well, we have a few days to prepare for the big night. In the meantime, I'm starving. Let's order dinner."

CHAPTER 20

TRAVIS

"Hey, do you want me to take you to work this morning?" I asked Claire over coffee on the deck.

Claire shook her head. "Nah. I'll be fine."

"Are you sure? I don't want Jill to give you a hard time when you walk through the door. I'd feel better if I was with you."

Claire reached across and trailed her fingers down my arm. "Thanks, but I'm a big girl. I can handle Jill. Her words may sting, but they won't kill me." She chuckled. She leaned back in the chair, and her hair caught the rays from the morning sun. I loved how it glistened.

Her eyes were closed from the glare when I leaned in to kiss her. She jolted when she felt my lips on hers and then laughed. "You startled me."

"You are so beautiful. If you need me, call me, okay?"

She hooked her arms around my neck. "I will, and thanks. Now come on; we need to get ready for work, and Tilly needs to go out."

It almost killed me to wait until lunchtime to call her. I held my phone with bated breath. I was eager to hear how her morning went. After three rings, I finally heard her sweet voice, and she sounded okay.

"Hey, babe. How's it going?' Claire asked.

"I'm good, but I'm calling to see how it went with Jill. She's not giving you a hard time, is she?'

"As a matter of fact, no, she's not. When I came in this morning, she had her arms crossed in front of her chest, which she always does when she has an attitude, and just nodded when I walked by. I said hi, but I don't know if she responded. I didn't hear her. I think she just nodded again and went back to her computer. I've not spoken to her since, and as usual, she's gone out for lunch with Sadie somewhere, so I don't have to deal with her in the break room."

I released an enormous sigh. "Well, that's a relief. It worried me all morning, and I hated that I wasn't there to defend you."

"I'm fine. I said everything that I needed to last night. If she chooses not to speak to me, that's her choice. It's how it's always been, anyway."

"Okay. Well, I'm glad to hear everything's okay. I'm going to call Slater and tell him we're on for dinner Saturday night." I paused for a second. "You're still okay with it, right?" I asked.

"Yes, I am." She released a nervous laugh.

"What's funny?"

"Oh, nothing. We seem to move forward in all kinds of directions."

"What do you mean? Is that a good or a bad thing?"

She heard the worry in my voice and soon put it to rest with another subtle laugh. "Oh, it's all good. I'm now talking to my parents' thanks to you. Jill finally knows about us, and we don't have to hide us anymore. As uncomfortable as it might be for a while, you can come to work anytime, and now Sabela and Slater are ready to accept us as a couple and want to be friends."

I smiled. She was right, and her words were comforting. "It will only get better from here, honey," I told her. "I'll see you tonight." I smiled to myself again as I thought about what I had with Claire. "Oh, and Claire."

"What?"

"I love you."

I heard the smile in her voice when she replied, and it warmed my heart. "I love you too, Travis. Bye."

After I ended the call, I immediately called Slater. He told me he was at the park with Sabela and Scottie, which explained the noise of kids playing in the background. I then wondered if I would ever experience the joy of taking a child of mine, whether it be biological or adopted, to a playground. I was sure Claire and I would find a way to have a family of our own.

"Is everything okay over at the house?" Slater asked. He quickly changed the subject. "Man, Scottie has no fear, I swear. He's climbing everything there is to climb here. We can't keep up with him. You wait, man. You'll know what I'm talking about someday."

I forced a laugh into the phone. "Sounds like you have your hands full."

"Oh, he keeps us busy, that's for sure. But he's settling in well. He calls me Daddy, which I just can't hear enough of, and he calls Sabela, Sabbie, which is cute. Sabela likes it, and I've even called her it a few times too." He let out a heavy, happy sigh. "Having a family is the best feeling in the world, Travis. It's so fulfilling and rewarding, and I'm so damn proud of Scottie. He reminds me so much of myself when I was a kid."

"I can't wait to meet him, which is why I'm calling. Claire and I would love to come over for dinner. Your invite touched her, and she wants to fix things between all of us just like you guys are willing to do."

"Great! I'll let Sabela know. Is six good?" he asked.

"Yeah, that will be fine."

"Okay. We will see you then. I have to run. Sabela is holding the fort, and Scottie is sure moving fast."

After hanging up the call, I tried to shake the feelings of jealousy that I had with Slater and his newfound son. I wanted what he had and feared I never would. I remembered feeling just as envious with the relationship he has with Sabela. I never thought I would ever get that lucky. Well, now I have that too with Claire. I guess you never know what life will hand you. I will never give up the dream of having a family with her someday; that's for sure.

After spending the rest of the afternoon at the job site, I called Claire again to ask what she wanted to do about dinner. She told me she had it under control and to come straight home. I was already feeling tired and thankful I wouldn't have to make any stops at the store and quickly got on the road for the thirty-minute drive home.

I was greeted at the door by an excited Tilly but also by the aroma of what promised to be a delicious home-cooked meal. I heard loud music coming from the kitchen, and it was obvious Claire hadn't heard me come through the front door. Blocked by Tilly at the entrance, I played with her for a few minutes until she tired herself out and returned to her bed. After setting down my ice chest, I headed to the kitchen and smiled at what I saw.

I stood in the doorway, unnoticed by Claire, and grinned. She was dressed in what I recognized to be one of my plaid shirts with the sleeves rolled up. Her legs and feet were bare, and I couldn't tell if she was or wasn't wearing underwear. *God, how sexy would that be if she weren't?* I continued to watch her as she swayed her body to the beat of the music and sang along out loud as she stirred something in a pot on the stove. I leaned against the doorjamb and enjoyed the view for a moment. I watched as she wriggled her ass from side to side; the shirt teased me by just hanging below her butt cheeks, revealing only the essence of her skin each time she gave her hips a good jolt. But it was enough for me to have to adjust the swelling in my jeans between my legs. I couldn't contain myself and had to say something. "Damn, I'm one hell of a lucky man."

Claire almost jumped out of her skin as she quickly turned around to face me, "Shit! You scared the crap out of me. How long have you been standing there?"

"Long enough to get a hard-on." I hollered over the sound of the music. I held out my arms. "Come over here and give me a kiss."

She fluttered her eyelids and did a catwalk stride over to me. "You're good at being sneaky," she said in a luring voice. Her pinky touched her lip. "I'm going to have to watch out for you."

I took her in my arms and kissed her passionately. "Yes, you will. When you think you are alone, you may not be."

She laughed and gave me a friendly slap on the chest. "I'm cooking you dinner. It should be ready soon."

We moved to the beat of the music as we stood in the middle of the kitchen embraced. "I smelled it as soon as I walked in. It smells fantastic. What are you fixing?" I asked.

She beamed me a cute smile. "Leg of lamb with all the fixings."

I smacked my lips. "Hmm, Yummy." I then reached up under her shirt and squeezed her bare ass. "You're not wearing any underwear. Damn, that's sexy." I said before planting another kiss on her lips. This time it lingered, and we danced in circles, keeping our lips locked.

"What's the occasion?" I asked with my arms tight around her waist.

"You." She said, followed by another smile.

I chuckled. "Me?"

"Yes, you. You've done so much for me over the last few months, and I just wanted to do something for you."

I pressed my body against hers and moved my hips to the beat of the music. She matched my rhythm and pulled me in tight. We kissed hard for a few minutes until Claire pulled away, heaving.

"Okay, if we keep this up, dinner will be burnt," she whispered as she freed herself from my hold.

Claire had gone all out and set the dining room table with her grandmother's silver candle holders. "I've never used these." She confessed, still panting. She lit the three candles and poured two glasses of wine. "You are the first person I've ever had for a home-cooked meal, so I wanted to honor my grandmother and use her dishes."

"I'm flattered. They're beautiful."

Claire took my hand and pulled out a chair with the other. "Now, you sit right here while I bring out dinner."

"Don't you want a hand?" I asked.

"Nope. It's my treat."

I raised my hands in defeat. "Okay. You win."

I watched as she returned to the kitchen, admiring her well-toned legs and the teasing of the shirt again.

A few minutes later, she appeared with two plates of steaming food and placed one in front of me. "Here you go."

"Oh man, this looks fantastic." I looked up and smiled. "You can cook too."

"Only when I want to," she laughed. "Which, as you've probably figured out, is not too often."

I was already chewing on a piece of lamb and had just arrived in heaven. "Oh man, this is so good. Thank you, baby."

"You're welcome." And then she circled her lips with her tongue. "After dinner, you are my dessert, in case you were wondering."

My eyes grew wide, and I froze while chewing my food. "Baby, you can have as much dessert as you want."

"Oh, honey, I intend to. I'm going to save a lot of room for dessert. I'm going to take care of you as much as you have taken care of me."

I wet my lips, leaned back in my chair, and admired her from across the table. No longer was there a haunting tension in the air. We held no secrets to Jill. That thought no longer existed, and it was noticeable tonight. We relaxed freely and felt the passion of our love. I wasn't about to break the mood and tell her I had spoken to Slater. Tonight it needed to be about my beautiful woman and me. The rest of the world can wait.

CHAPTER 21

CLAIRE

After spoiling Travis with a home-cooked meal, I kept my promise and continued the trend in bed. I teased, kissed, and caressed every inch of his magnificent body, which left him breathless and me hopelessly in love. Last night he was my world, and I made sure he knew it. I seduced him with my tongue, my mouth, my fingers, and my entire body. We made love for hours and only forced ourselves to stop because our jobs would call us in the morning.

When I woke the next morning, I was still curled in Travis's arms just like I was when we fell asleep. I took in a deep breath and drowned my sinuses with his scent. God, he smelled good. I felt his warm breath next to my ear, and then I heard him whisper. "Good morning, beautiful."

I pulled his arm tighter over my chest and kissed the rough skin on his arm. "Hey, good morning. You're awake."

He kissed the top of my head. "I've been awake for a while. I didn't want to wake you."

I rolled my naked body until I faced him and gave him a radiant smile. "How did you sleep?" I asked.

"Thanks to you and the amazing love session, I slept like a baby."

I giggled and buried my face into his chest. "Me, too. I don't want to go to work today. I just want to lie here all day in bed with you."

"If Slater didn't show up at nine, I'd say let's play hooky." He glanced at the clock on the end table. "In fact, I'd better get my lazy ass in the shower."

"I'd join you, but then I'd be late for work too because I won't be able to resist you," I admired his naked body as he left the room and thought he was perfect in every way. A few minutes later, I heard Tilly's ritual morning bark and reluctantly pulled myself out of bed to make coffee and take her outside. "Coming, Tilly!" I hollered as I grabbed my bathrobe.

We had two days until our dinner with Slater and Sabela. I wasn't sure what to expect or how the evening would pan out, but as the day drew closer, my nerves peaked. Travis tuned in to my nervous energy and tried his best to comfort me with his words, but they weren't going away that easily.

Friday after work, I stopped at the market and bought all the ingredients I needed to make a strawberry cheesecake when I got home, so it would have enough time to set in the fridge before we were to leave at five.

I spent Saturday afternoon going through my entire closet, wondering what to wear. I don't get invited to dinners too often and didn't know what the protégé was for dinner with friends. Travis was of no help. "Just wear what you're comfortable in," he uttered.

"That would be my sweats. I don't think so," I laughed. I didn't own many dresses, and the ones I had felt too overdressed with their flowers and lace. I'd probably only worn them once for some special occasion and had shoved them in the back of my closet, never to see daylight again. I finally settled on a pair of jeans, a light blue V-neck shirt, and a beige fringed suede vest. For shoes, I chose knee-high leather boots, which I tucked my jeans into.

I kept my make-up light but wore a little more jewelry than I'm used to, so I wouldn't feel so much like a plain Jane next to Sabela. She always looked spectacular in anything she wore—even her dental assistant scrubs.

After giving myself one last look in the full-length mirror, I smiled at myself and whispered to my reflection. "Okay, let's do this."

Travis entered the room. He smelled divine and dressed sharply in a pair of brand new jeans and a black shirt which he had unbuttoned just enough to tease, "Wow, you look fantastic," he uttered. He stood behind me and wrapped me in his arms. "I love the boots."

I turned to face him and gave him a tender kiss on the lips. "Thanks. You look and smell delicious."

He kept me in his arms. "So, are we ready to do this?" he asked.

"As ready as I'll ever be." I broke away from his hold. "I just need to feed Tilly."

Ten minutes later, we were on our way. Travis drove while I held the cheesecake carefully on my lap.

"How are you doing?" Travis asked. "We'll be there in five minutes." He added.

I turned and gave him a genuine smile. "I'm doing okay. I thought by now I'd be wanting to turn around and go home. But that's not the case. I want this to go well, and I honestly have a feeling it will."

Travis nodded and returned the smile. "Me too. I think we're all going to be just fine." He said as he reached over and squeezed my shoulder.

When we stood at their front door, Travis gave me a reassuring smile. "Ready?" he asked.

I took a deep breath and nodded. "Yes."

Travis rang the doorbell, and I felt my heart rate rise just a notch, but it soon returned to normal when Slater opened the door and greeted us with a warm, friendly smile that washed all my worries away. He opened the door wide to invite us into his home and gave Travis a friendly pat on the shoulder as he shook his hand. "Hey, man. Glad you could make it. Come on in," he said as he stepped back and gestured with his arms.

He then focused his eyes on me and again smiled, "Claire. Welcome to our home. Sabela and Scottie are in the kitchen."

I gave him a nervous smile. "Thank you." and held out the dessert. "I made a cheesecake."

Slater took it from my hands. "Ooh, one of my favorites. How did you know?" he said jokingly.

Once my hands were free, I quickly grabbed one of Travis's, and he immediately gave it a hard squeeze, followed by a beautiful smile. Slater closed the door behind us and led us over to the kitchen on the left, where we found Sabela and Scottie sitting at the table. Scottie was sitting on her lap listening to Sabela read him a book. The aroma of something delicious cooking in the oven filled the condo. The table had been set for four and saucepans steamed on the stovetop.

"Travis, Claire, I want you to meet my son Scottie," he laughed. "No, sorry, *our* son."

Sabela lifted Scottie off her lap and onto the floor. He immediately raced over to Slater, who picked him up and kissed him on the cheek. There was no doubt they were father and son. They looked so much alike. From the dark curly hair, the deep blue eyes and even the dimple on his cheek when he smiled was an exact match to Slaters.

"Wow, he looks just like you," Travis said as he approached Scottie and took his tiny hand. "Hey, buddy. It's good to meet you finally."

Sabela joined Slater and wrapped her arm around his waist. She was dressed casually in jeans and a cute purple top, which made me glad I hadn't worn one of my ugly lace dresses.

"Can you say hi, Scottie? This is Travis," Sabela said.

Scottie tucked his head into the crook of his dad's neck and quietly said, "Hi."

"Aww, since when have you've been shy." Slater laughed.

Sabela then looked at me and made me feel at ease when she gave me a friendly smile, "And this is Claire."

I took Scottie's hand. "Hi, Scottie."

Scottie remained shy and quietly said, "Hi." again.

"He is beautiful and looks so much like you, Slater. You must be very proud," I said.

"Oh, I am." He turned and gave Sabela a peck on the cheek. "These two are my world," he said as he sat Scottie down. "Go on, buddy. Why don't you play with your cars while Sabbie and I get dinner ready?"

We all stood in the kitchen and watched with warm hearts as Scottie raced over to his chest in the open-planned living room and pulled out some toys.

"He's beautiful," Travis said. "Congratulations, man."

"Thanks. It will be your turn someday." He pulled out a chair at the table. "Here, have a seat, and I'll grab you a beer. Claire, would you like a beer?"

"Sure, that would be great, thanks." I said as I took a seat next to Travis and held his hand."

"Honey, do you want one?" he asked Sabela, who had walked over to Scottie and was kneeling next to him.

"Yes, please. Dinner won't be ready for another twenty minutes. I'll join you after I've put some cartoons on for Scottie. He has already eaten and will be ready for bed soon."

Sabela left Scottie to watch the TV and joined us at the table where she took a seat next to Slater. I gulped down some of my beer before I found the courage to speak. I looked at Sabela and smiled. "Thank you for having us. This means a lot."

Sabela returned the friendly smile. "It's something we should have done a long time ago. I'm sorry for how I've treated you because of what your brother did to me. You are not to blame, and it was wrong of me. I hope you can find it in your heart to forgive me."

Sabela's words left a lump in my throat. I wasn't expecting such a sincere apology from her, and it moved me close to tears. Slater and Travis held our hands tight but remained silent as we exchanged words.

"Sabela, thank you," I said, my eyes now misty. "That means a lot. I'm so sorry for what my brother did to you, and because of the monster that he is, I no longer consider him family."

"I know Claire. Travis told me, and that's when I realized how wrong I had been. I know we didn't hang out much when I worked at the dentist's office, but I'd like to change that. You and Travis are a couple now, and I want to get to know you if you'd let me."

I was stunned that Sabela asked my permission to be her friend. For so long, I had felt intimidated by her beauty and perfection only to find out she is the kindest person and speaks from the heart. "I would love that."

"Sabela reached across the table and took my free hand, great. Do you want to help me get dinner ready?"

I was pleased she had asked and rose to my feet. "Sure. I would love to."

Sabela had fixed roast beef and vegetables, and while she carved and served up the meat, she had me finish up the gravy and heat some rolls. We said a few words, but the mood was comfortable, and we both knew we were off to a wonderful start to build what I hoped would be a good friendship.

Travis and Slater remained seated at the table and talked about Eve's house and the progress they had made. By the time dinner was ready, Scottie had moved to Slater's lap.

Over dinner, the conversation was casual. Most of it focused on Scottie and how Sabela and Slater were enjoying their new roles as parents. We were all captivated by him, mesmerized by the overload of cuteness that sat before us. I was envious of what they had and knew Travis was too, and for the first time, I felt the need to say something when Sabela returned from putting Scottie to bed.

"I swear he is the easiest kid to put to sleep." She said as she grabbed herself another beer from the fridge. "Does anyone else want one?" she asked before closing the door.

"Nope, I just got three new ones for us," Slater said as he raised his bottle.

Sabela rejoined us. She leaned back in her chair and took a swig of her beer. "Do you want children someday, Claire?"

I couldn't hide the sudden sadness that masked my face, and Sabela saw it too and showed signs of uneasiness as she shifted in her seat. "I'm sorry. I didn't mean to ask such a personal question.," she said with flushed cheeks.

With sad eyes, I looked over at Travis for a moment and then back at Sabela. "I can't have children."

Sabela gasped and brought her hand up to her dropped jaw. "Oh, Claire, I'm so sorry. I didn't know."

Travis leaned over and draped his arm over my shoulder. I reached up and held his hand before giving him a loving smile. "It's okay. How could you know? I haven't told anyone except Travis."

Slater leaned forward. "Man, I'm so sorry, guys."

Travis rubbed my shoulder as he spoke. "It's okay. We're not ruling out the possibility of fertility drugs or even adoption. Claire and I have spent hours talking about our future together, and one way or another, there will be children in it." Travis released a slight laugh and curled his lip. "Remember when I told you guys that you two had the real deal and that I hoped someday I would too. "Well, I've found it man with Claire. What we have is the real deal, and no matter what the future holds, we will be in it together. I love her with all my heart."

Slater nodded. "I see it. Your eyes light up when you say her name. Just like mine do when I say Sabela." He turned to Sabela and gave her a playful wink.

Sabela blew him a kiss and then looked my way. "So, there is still a possibility that you can have children if you used fertility drugs?" she asked with hope in her voice.

I shrugged my shoulders. "Maybe. From what I understand, there's a lot of testing involved. I've never considered it an option until I met Travis. I'm sure it's something we will look into, and as he said, adoption is another option."

Sabela hesitated before she spoke. "Please tell me if it's none of my business, but wouldn't you prefer to try the fertility drug method first and try to have kids of your own versus adopting?"

Travis looked at me and gave my shoulder a sharp squeeze before answering her question. "Most couples would probably want to try that route first, but I know neither one of you knew that I grew up moving from place to place in foster care. I never knew my parents. So for me adopting one or more children would prevent them from going through what I went through, and it's just as important as trying to have our own." Travis turned to face me and smiled. "Claire gets it and agrees."

At that very moment, I had never been so proud of Travis, and my misty eyes told him I was. He didn't have to tell Slater and Sabela about his upbringing, but I understood why he had. It was to support me. I had shared a very private part about myself, and Travis thought it was only right he should do the same and explain why we would be okay with adoption.

Suddenly Slater beamed a huge smile and took Sabela's hand. "Can I talk to you for a minute in private?" he asked Sabela.

Sabela looked uncomfortable with his request and looked at me with apologetic eyes. "Honey, we have guests. Can't it wait?"

Slater grinned, which offended me. I didn't see any reason for him to be smiling, and then he had the nerve to request to talk to Sabela in private. It was also troublesome. What couldn't he say in front of us? I had just shared with him a secret I had held for many years, and now he wants to be secretive. I tried not to act upset when he took Sabela's hand.

"This will only take a minute. I promise." He said, still smiling, He stood before Sabela and pulled her to her feet. I watched as he led her out of the dining area and up the stairs.

I was a little tweaked and let Travis know. "Well, that was odd. I guess there are some things Slater doesn't want us to know," I said before taking a sip of beer.

Travis shook his head and spat his words. "Yeah, after we just poured our hearts out to him." He leaned forward and rolled his eyes. "Now, I kinda wished we hadn't."

I took a large gulp of my drink. "Is it me? Or do you think it's rude of Slater? I mean, I thought we were trying to build a friendship here. Last I heard, friends don't keep secrets from one another."

Travis leaned back and rested his hands behind his head. "I have no idea what's going on, but I'm getting pissed." He reached for his beer and took a swig. "I mean, this is bullshit. What's taking them so damn long. What the hell is he telling her?"

"Maybe he doesn't want to be friends with me. I mean, after all, it was my brother that tried to rape his fiancée. Maybe he thought he could handle being around me but has realized I'm just a reminder of the terrible things Davin did to Sabela."

Travis shook his head. "Nah, that's not it. They told me before I lived with you how they had moved on and put all that behind them."

The sound of footsteps coming from the top of the stairs jolted me from my relaxed state, and I gave Travis a sharp tap on the knee. "Shh, I hear them coming," I whispered.

Slater returned, still wearing the smirk which had annoyed me. I wanted to reach up and wipe it off his face. I glanced at Sabela for any inclination on what they had talked about but saw she was smiling too. I was not amused. I looked away and folded my arms as they remained standing and held hands.

"Everything okay? Travis asked with a creased brow.

"Couldn't be better," Slater said with an even bigger grin.

I didn't like all the secrecy and sneered at him through my gritted teeth.

He turned and looked at Sabela as he spoke. "Sabela and I have a proposition for you both."

"You do?" Travis asked with his brow still creased.

Slater looked our way. "We do. It's about Eve's house."

Travis glanced at me for a second, looking puzzled. "What about Eve's house? Which is yours now, by the way." Travis said.

Slater chuckled at Travis's reminder. "Yeah, I know, but it still feels weird to call it mine. Anyway, my first idea was to donate it to The Children of America." He shook his head slightly and smiled again. "It's funny how we all want to help fostered kids?" Slater said, and after my brief talk with Sabela, I think we've come up with a better idea."

Travis rested his hands in front of him on the table. "Okay, what did you decide?"

He paused and gave Sabela another smile, and she nodded. Slater beamed an enormous grin when he spoke. "We've decided that we will keep the house and turn it into a children's home, and we would like you and Claire to be in charge of it."

CHAPTER 22

CLAIRE

My anger quickly dissolved, and I gasped, shocked by what I had just heard. Stunned by their proposal, I had no words. Two hours ago, I didn't know if we could even be friends, and now, they are entrusting us with a proposition that could change mine and Travis's lives forever.

I looked at Travis. His dropped jaw and silence mirrored how I felt. We were speechless.

"Well?" Slater said without losing his grin.

Travis spoke with the widest eyes I had ever seen. "Are you serious? You'd want us to run the home for you and take care of the children?"

I searched for my words. "I don't know what to say. That's an enormous responsibility," I finally replied.

Slater took a seat while Sabela grabbed four more beers from the fridge. Slater's eyes were as wide as mine and Travis's, and he couldn't hide the enthusiasm in his voice. "Look, guys. I don't know anything about opening a children's home or what permits we need, but if we can do it, I'm willing to give it a shot. After listening to your stories, you guys have the hearts to give love and provide a loving home to those kids, where society and the foster care system has failed them."

My heart melted when I saw Travis wipe his eyes. "I don't know what to say, man. For me, it would be a dream come true. I've always wanted to help at least one kid and save him or her from the ruts of adoption, but to save a house full and be a father figure to all of them would be an amazing feeling." He turned to me and took my hand. "What do you say, Claire?"

My head was spinning with this life-changing opportunity, but I listened to my heart and not my head. "Yes!" I squealed as streams of happy tears began gushing down my cheeks.

Travis jumped to his feet and pulled me up out of my chair. "Yes! You said, yes!" He roared as he spun me around.

I nodded and laughed out loud as Travis continued to dance around the room with me. "You said, yes!" He bellowed and then looked me in the eyes. "Are you sure, Claire? We can go home and think about it."

I tried to stop the tears of happiness but failed. "I don't need to think about it. Yes, I'm sure." I broke free of Travis's embrace and turned to face Sabela and Slater, who were standing arm in arm, holding each other tight. I wiped my eyes as I approached them, and they welcomed me into a group hug. "Thank you so much for this opportunity and for believing in Travis and me. We won't let you down. I promise."

Travis joined us and gave Slater and Sabela each a hug. "I'll do whatever you need me to do to make this happen, and Claire and I will help you any way we can." He said with watery eyes before taking me in his arms again.

"Well, right now, it's an idea, but I know together as a team we can do this," Slater said. "It's going to be a full-time job to put all of this together and do the research and do it right," he added.

I didn't hesitate with my next words. "I'll quit my job tomorrow." I quickly said. "I hate it there. Especially now that Jill knows about Travis and me. And I will take any courses that are required to run a children's home." I wanted this just as much as Travis did. We'd love and raise all the children as if they were our own. For me, this would be so much more rewarding than going through the endless fertility drug tests that may end up failing and not to mention heartbreaking. Travis took me in his arms and held me tight. His eyes glazed with tears.

Sabela touched my arm. "Wait, you said Jill knows about you guys. How long has she known? I've not seen her since the day after you broke up. I've been so busy with Scottie. I haven't called her."

"Just a few days. When Travis decided on a whim to show up at my work and tell Jill about us," I said. "She has a new roommate now, Sadie. She's the new girl at work, and they hang out with each other all the time now. I wouldn't worry about not being able to call her. She's doing fine."

Sabela suddenly looked worried. "Hey, wait a minute. Does she know I knew about you guys, and I kept it from her? If she does, then I need to explain to her why I did."

I shrugged my shoulders. "I don't think so. Your name never came up."

"Well, that's a relief," Sabela said as she let her body relax. "But even so, I should call her and make things right. She's always been a good friend, and it still haunts me that I kept a secret from her, but it wasn't my job to tell her." She took a deep breath. "Look, I know we've all had bumpy roads to get to this point. A lot has happened that caused friction between us, but I'm speaking for Slater and me. We're hoping that we can all move forward, including Jill—if she accepts my apology and can put everything behind us and start fresh." She glanced at Slater and gave him a loving smile. "We would love to have all of you at our wedding, including Jill. Which is another reason I need to call her?"

Before I could reply to Sabela's touching speech, Travis turned to face me and smiled before getting down on one knee. "There's something I want to say first," he said.

I gasped and held both my hands up to my face to cover my dropped jaw. "Travis, what are you doing?"

He laughed and gave me his famous sexy smile. "Claire. If we're going to have a house full of kids that will look up to us for love and guidance, then I want to make it official." He gave me that smile again, and I gave him a nervous laugh. "Claire, will you marry me?" I don't have a ring, but it's coming soon, I promise."

Sabela and Slater were smiling while locked in an embrace as they anxiously waited for my answer.

"Oh my god, Travis." I cried. "Yes! Yes, I will marry you."

Travis jumped up from his knee and took me in his arms and spun me around to the sound of applause from Sabela and Slater. "I love you so much," Travis said as he planted a long kiss on my lips.

"I love you too." I managed to say between my tears of bliss before I locked my arms around his neck and kissed him hard on the lips.

"Oh my god, this is so beautiful," Sabela said. "Now, we have two weddings to plan."

I laughed at the thought. "Yes, we do. I'll help you guys if you help us."

"Deal," Sabela said as she embraced me. "Congratulations, Claire. I'm so happy for you both."

"Thank you, Sabela. Thank you for everything."

"Don't thank me, okay. Slater and I did the right thing." She pulled away and then looked at me with questionable eyes. "We will have to talk to Jill. I had asked her to help me plan my wedding when Slater first proposed to me."

My jaw dropped. "We?" I stuttered. "I, I don't think she's going to want to help me plan my wedding, Sabela. I'm marrying her ex-boyfriend, remember?'

Sabela waved her arms. "But it sounds like she's moved on. Maybe I am thinking the impossible, and she will laugh in my face." Sabela released a devious smile while the guys listened in on what Sabela was conjuring up. "But after I have made amends, I'm going to talk to her about your wedding."

She grabbed my hands and folded them into hers. "I think it would be wonderful if we could all be friends and plan our weddings together. What do you think?"

I wasn't sure how to react. "Ha! I think you're crazy, Sabela. It will never happen. But hey, give it your best shot. I'm game."

Sabela's devious smile returned. "Never say never, Claire. It will happen. You and I are going to have a hell of a wedding, and I can't wait to get started on planning them."

ALSO BY TINA HOGAN GRANT

THE TAMMY MELLOWS SERIES
Reckless Beginnings - Book 1
Better Endings - Book 2
The Reunions Books 3

THE SABELA SERIES
Davin - Prequel
Slater - Book 1
Eve - Book 2
Claire - Book 3
Jill - Book 4

Want to be the first to know when Tina has a new release?
Sign up to stay in the loop

Visit the author's website
https://www.tinahogangrant.com
Join Tina's Facebook Group – Read More Books

ABOUT THE AUTHOR

Tina Hogan Grant loves to write stories with strong female characters that know what they want and aren't afraid to chase their dreams. She loves to write sexy and sometimes steamy romances with happy ever after endings.

She is living life to the fullest in a small mountain community in Southern California with her husband and two dogs. When she is not writing she is probably riding her ATV, kayaking or hiking with her best friend – her husband of twenty-five years.

www.tinahogangrant.com

WHERE CAN YOU FIND TINA?
Join her Facebook Reading Group where she does live chats,

cover reveals, reads excerpts and does plenty of giveaways including signed ACR books.

FOLLOW HER ON THESE SOCIAL MEDIA ACCOUNTS

Made in the USA
Monee, IL
18 September 2021